He leaned over and kissed Jenny. His lips felt cold and tasted salty, but they warmed quickly, sending pleasant thrills along Jenny's spine. Droplets of sea spray slid from his hair onto her nose.

"I've missed you, Jenny," he whispered.

"Me, too," she answered softly. She reached out a tentative hand to smooth his damp, boisterous curls.

"Jenny . . ." His eyes held her own. "I don't intend to be a secret any longer. From now on I'll do all my admiring up front. . . ."

Dear Readers,

We at Silhouette would like to thank all our readers for your many enthusiastic letters. In direct response to your encouragement, we are now publishing *four* FIRST LOVEs every month.

As always FIRST LOVEs are written especially for and about you—your hopes, your dreams, your ambitions.

Please continue to share your suggestions and comments with us; they play an important part in our pleasing you.

I invite you to write to us at the address below:

Nancy Jackson
Senior Editor
Silhouette Books
P.O. Box 769
New York, N.Y. 10019

SECRET
ADMIRER
Carrie Enfield

First Love from Silhouette

Published by Silhouette Books New York

America's Publisher of Contemporary Romance

Other First Loves by Carrie Enfield

Songbird
Picture Perfect

SILHOUETTE BOOKS, a Division of Simon & Schuster, Inc
1230 Avenue of the Americas, New York, N.Y. 10020

Copyright © 1983 by Carrie Enfield

Distributed by Pocket Books

ISBN: 0-671-53362-2

First Silhouette Books printing September, 1983

10 9 8 7 6 5 4 3 2 1

America's Publisher of Contemporary Romance

Printed in the U.S.A.

*Special thanks to junior volunteer
Kevin Wait of Community Hospital, Santa Cruz,
for his valuable help.*

SECRET
ADMIRER

1

Clear the way!"

The thin wail of a siren was followed by barked orders, then the emergency entrance doors thudded open. Flaxen-haired Jennifer Carlson looked up from her filing in the inner office, and ventured out into the hall to see what was coming in.

Jenny was a new candy striper, and she'd never worked in the emergency room until tonight. Everyone warned her that Friday night was the busiest time, and there was a waiting room already full of people with various complaints. But nothing serious, until now.

Her heart caught in her throat at the sight of the ashen-faced boy on the stretcher, flanked by attendants. Jenny guessed he was about her own age, fifteen, or maybe a little older. His chestnut curls lay in wet tendrils across his broad forehead, and his eyes, meeting hers, were a startled blue.

"Hi," he said, his voice deep and resonant.

"Hi." She smiled.

The moment passed as the boy was quickly surrounded by nurses and a doctor. Another boy, who was wheeled in after him, didn't appear so badly injured. The emergency room doors closed behind them, and Jenny suddenly remembered her filing.

Dutifully, she bent over the files, her light, shoulder-length hair veiling her face.

"His leg's broken. Better get him down to X-ray."

"Just try to relax, Brian. Everything's going to be okay," a nurse assured the first boy as he was wheeled down to X-ray. Jenny noticed how tense his jaw looked, as though he were clenching up against the pain, which had to be very bad. A flood of sympathy overtook her.

"Looks in pretty bad shape, doesn't he?" Skip Trybom, a nursing attendant, leaned an arm against the gray metal cabinet. "I think they were in a car wreck."

"Really? That's awful!" Jenny took in Skip's appearance—tall, lanky, with high-arched brows on a boyish face. His dark kinky hair was a direct contrast to his starched whites. Having graduated from high school a year early at seventeen, Skip was now working his way through college. He was one of those people who loved the hands-on type of work with patients, and he and Jenny found they got along together famously.

A few minutes later, the other boy walked into the hallway. He had a small bandage wrapped around one wrist and a Band-Aid on his cheek.

Shelly Fleming, Jenny's best friend, waved at her from the doorway, then made faces to get Jenny's attention on the boy.

"Hey, Jay Sheldon. What happened to you . . . or should I ask?" Shelly gasped as if she'd just told the joke of the century.

That was Shelly—always wisecracking, even at the wrong times. At five foot two, with bright copper hair and sea-green eyes, Shelly had a mouth to compensate for any lack of size. She loved to joke and flirt with boys, and generally be silly, which made her a lot of fun to be around. Patients either loved her or cringed when they saw her coming, but very few forgot her. She was the sister of Jenny's boyfriend, Steve.

Jay Sheldon tossed his mop of thick brown hair and smiled grimly at Shelly. "You wouldn't believe it . . . it was so bad. My friend Brian Halsey was with me, driving along the coast. You know him?"

Shelly shook her head, wide-eyed.

"Anyway, my van was hit by another car and we rolled down a small embankment. Brian's leg's broken. He's down in X-ray right now, poor guy."

"What about you?" Shelly motioned to his bandaged wrist.

"Oh, this is nothing. Just a sprain. Brian's the one I'm worried about."

"That's terrible," breathed Shelly.

"Brian Halsey . . . he's the track champ, isn't he?" Skip asked.

Skip stood close to Jenny while she tried to concentrate on her filing. She had the funny feeling he might like her, for he'd been showing her a lot more attention lately. Of course, they shared the common interest of the hospital, but if he did like her, how would she handle it?

Problems like that never seemed to plague Shelly, who could flirt with guys easily, even during a disaster like this. She was naturally friendly, and thought nothing of approaching someone and striking up a conversation.

It wasn't that way for Jenny, although she never considered herself shy. She was just "reserved"—she guessed that was the right word. Most of the time, it was difficult for her to find the right place to begin a conversation. With patients, she'd learned to ask them about their interests, and a conversation usually sprang from there. But she knew that if Skip liked her as more than a friend, she'd tend to freeze up in his presence.

That never happened with Steve, of course. With Steve, Jenny could talk about school and surfing—Steve's hobby—and they always had something to talk about. Sometimes, she sensed that Steve was more interested in surfing than in her, but it didn't bother her. She had her own interests, and besides, Shelly said that a lot of surfers were that way, practically married to the sea.

Also, Jenny enjoyed watching him ride the waves. He was as graceful as a ballerina, balanced precariously on his board as it sliced through the water. She liked sitting down on the cliffs in the early morning, with a Thermos of coffee, bundled in her ski jacket, waiting for him to come clambering up the rocks to her side.

Steve Fleming was Jenny's first real boyfriend. She'd been on two casual dates before, but they didn't really count. A boyfriend was different—someone you got to know really well, someone to share with, someone who wanted to take you out every weekend. Now that she knew what it was like, she liked the security.

But in the beginning, Jenny had had a hard time getting Steve to notice her as a real girl, since he just thought of her as one of his sister's friends. She had to find the time to talk to him when Shelly wasn't around, because Shelly was bound to blurt out something embarrassing—that's how she was. So Jenny started going over to his house early, knowing Shelly wouldn't be home yet.

Usually, Steve was in the garage, working on his surfboard or motorcycle.

"Do you know how this works?" he'd ask her, and then he'd launch into a detailed explanation of how different motorcycle parts worked.

"It's sort of like a body," Jenny observed.

Steve laughed. "Yeah, except you can't get

new parts for a body when the old ones wear out."

"Science is working on it," Jenny shot back.

She remembered that the second time she talked to him in the garage, he'd looked at her for a long time, as if he were seeing her differently. "Why are you staring at me?" she asked him finally.

"Because I never really looked at you before."

Then he asked her out, and they'd been together ever since.

"Jenny, I think you're all finished for tonight. It's ten on the dot." Debbie Michaels, a night-shift nurse, smiled at her, rearranging her cap on her cropped auburn hair.

Jenny gathered up her coat and purse, and joined Shelly and Jay in the hall.

"You know Steve's gonna be late picking us up," Shelly said. "So let's go down to X-ray and see what's happening to Brian, okay?"

Jenny could tell her friend really wanted to spend more time with Jay Sheldon, so she agreed, walking just behind the couple.

Brian lay on a gurney outside the X-ray room, a strained smile on his lips. "Suspicion's confirmed. My leg's thoroughly broken —in more than one place."

"Geez, buddy. There goes the track season," Jay moaned, shaking his head mournfully.

"Don't I know it. Oh, well, maybe I'll become the season's star basketweaver, or something." Brian winked at Jenny, whose face flushed.

"I'm sorry," she said, not knowing whether it was right to smile or not. He was trying to be so upbeat about the whole disaster. "You're in track?"

"He's the guy we're counting on," Jay supplied, shaking his fist in the air.

Brian looked at Jenny while he talked. "They'll manage fine without me. I'm not indispensable, though I'd like to be remembered. And right now I'm not in the mood to think about running, gang." He forced the words through clenched teeth.

"Once they give you a shot, you'll feel a lot better," Jenny said.

"I know what it's like . . . I've broken a leg before," Skip said, wrapping his arm playfully around Jenny's shoulders. "Jenny here thinks she knows it all—her dad's a doctor."

Jenny blushed. "Yeah, sure, Skip. You know, the first person I'm going to do surgery on is you."

"Cut out his tongue, will you?" Shelly suggested.

"Take it easy, Brian," Jenny said softly as Skip wheeled him away. His eyes were so arresting, Jenny found it difficult to pull her gaze away from his.

She turned quickly and hurried to meet Steve. Under the fluorescent hospital lighting, Steve's sun-bleached blond hair contrasted sharply with his deep tan. Jenny wondered if that was the first thing other people noticed about him, or if another part of him caught their eye—his easy, loping gait; his friendly

15

brown eyes; or the ready, playful smile that lit up his whole face.

"It's about time!" shouted Shelly, waggling her rose-painted fingernails at Jay Sheldon. "See ya, Jay!"

"Sorry I'm late," Steve apologized, falling into step beside Jenny. "How'd it go?"

"Oh, fine. There was some excitement tonight." She told him about the accident.

Once they were settled in the car, Steve slipped his arm around Jenny. Usually he didn't do that in front of Shelly; she always had some smart remark to make. But tonight she kept quiet and stared dreamily out the back window—probably thinking about Jay.

"I've got some free Boardwalk tickets," Steve said. "Wanna go tomorrow night?"

"Oh, sure. I'd love to," Jenny answered.

"I'll call you tomorrow to let you know what time, okay?" He pulled the light blue Toyota into her driveway—a long, narrow, downhill road that turned to gravel in front of the Spanish-style house.

A red tile roof sloped over white stucco, which was partially hidden by overzealous vines. Windowboxes overflowed with bright blue lobelia, and pots of different sizes and shapes were clustered on the front porch.

Lights from inside sent filmy streamers across the gravel. Steve parked in the dark, under some honeysuckle bushes, and drew Jenny close, his lips brushing hers. "See you tomorrow, okay?"

"Okay." Jenny stepped out of the car, feeling spaced out.

Funny, Steve's kiss always had that effect on her—as if he could brush away any other thoughts she might have, just with the touch of his lips.

Jenny had forgotten that her younger sister, Brooke, was having a slumber party that night, so she was surprised by the squeals and hysterical laughter of four silly girls when she walked in the house.

Thirteen-year-old Brooke and her friends were making taffy in the kitchen, and Jenny's parents were in the den watching television with eight-year-old Thad and the family sheepdog, Woolly.

Jenny's mother emerged from the den to see what all the commotion was about.

"By now those girls could have taffy from one end of the kitchen to the other," she twittered, running into Jenny in the hall. "Oh, hi, Jen. How was your evening?"

"Fine," Jenny replied.

Her mom had been a registered nurse for several years, and was now working toward a degree in psychology. Besides that, she worked for charities, Cub Scouts, the soccer league, the ladies' auxiliary at the hospital— always busy with some activity. Dr. Carlson teased that her family had to make an appointment to speak with her.

Jenny followed her into the kitchen, watching her thread her fingers through her short, sandy hair in a gesture of good-natured exasperation.

"There was a car accident tonight. One of the boys broke his leg, but the other one came out of it with just a few scrapes," Jenny explained above the din of thirteen-year-old laughter.

Brooke was perched on the counter. Her friend, Christine Reese, backed up against the refrigerator door, a heavy, thick rope of taffy stretched between them.

"Who was in the accident?" Margie Gaines, another friend, asked.

"Jay Sheldon and Brian Halsey. I don't know them. They go to Aptos."

"Oh, Brian Halsey? My sister knows him." Christine giggled and shot meaningful looks at the other girls. "Is he okay?"

"His leg's broken, but he'll be okay," Jenny explained.

"Isn't he cute?"

"He's too old for you, Christine," Brooke cut in, and the others burst out laughing.

"Christine loves older men," cooed Connie Letterman, which elicited fresh chuckles.

Brooke slid off the counter and doubled over in laughter. Her white-blond hair was cut in a pixieish style, emphasizing her pert face—a younger version of Jenny's, except that her eyes were blue where Jenny's were light brown.

"Now keep your mind on this taffy," Maxine Carlson warned. "You girls are getting so

18

silly, you'll be swinging from the ceiling soon."

"Imagine what they'll be like when they reach my age—totally bananas," scoffed Jenny, taking a glass of orange juice to her room.

Jenny had decorated her room in white and yellow, with pin-striped curtains and matching bedspread. The pillows were different shades of yellow, sewn by Jenny herself. She loved how sunny the room seemed, even on a gloomy day. Sitting down in the old rocker her grandmother had left her, she stared at the photograph of Steve which sat on her dresser amid a crowd of family pictures.

He looked so handsome and grown-up for his senior picture, with his hair slicked down in place, his expression serious but sort of mysterious. No wonder lots of girls thought he was really a catch, Jenny thought proudly.

She finished her juice and went into the den.

"Hi, Dad. Hi, Thad."

"Oh, hi, pumpkin. Looks like we'll be getting very little sleep tonight with that mob, doesn't it?" her father greeted her.

"Ugh. Girls," grunted Thad, who was sprawled on the floor next to Woolly.

There was one small desk lamp on in the room, and Thad's head was outlined darkly against the TV screen. He was the one in the family who looked most like Mom, with his thick sandy hair, spattering of freckles, and slanted brown eyes in a wide, friendly face.

Jenny and Brooke got their coloring and light hair from Dr. Carlson, whose few wisps of pale blondness were combed across a growing bald spot. He liked to keep it covered with a variety of caps. Going bald, he explained, had given him a penchant for hats.

"They'll be up all night telling jokes, thinking they're hysterically funny," Jenny added. "The kitchen's a mess."

"The price they must pay for such fun is to clean up after themselves." Her dad chuckled. "How was your night?"

"Okay." She told her father about the accident.

"I remember them coming in," he said. "Funny we didn't run into each other. I had a small patient in emergency with an ear infection about that time."

"Was it real bloody?" inquired Thad.

"How gross, Thad," said Jenny. "Is that all you ever think about?"

"I do have a few other interests," he said in a Dracula voice, jutting his front teeth forward, making full use of his overbite.

He looked so funny, Jenny couldn't help laughing.

"Another future doctor in the family?" Dr. Carlson chuckled.

"Dr. Jekyll," joked Jenny.

"Actually, many of my patients are pretty bloodthirsty, like you, Thad. They like to know what's being done to them, although some prefer to close their eyes and pretend nothing's happening."

An uninvited picture of Brian Halsey floated into Jenny's mind. She wondered how he was doing. Was he in pain? Had he closed those incredible blue eyes to shut himself off from the sterile hospital world?

"What do you want to go on first? Bumper cars?" Steve grinned mischievously at Jenny.

The hurdy-gurdy music of the Boardwalk, mixed with screams and laughter and loud *whap-whaps* from the shooting gallery, filled the air. Popcorn, cotton candy and taffy aromas assaulted Jenny's nose, stirring her hunger even though she'd just eaten.

"Sounds good," Jenny said. Steve slipped his hand in hers and a tingle traveled up her arm, filling her with excitement.

They each chose a bumper car. Jenny loved them, careening around the slippery floor, trying to smash into Steve. They counted how many times each other hit—Steve: 12, Jenny: 7.

"Now the roller coaster," Steve suggested, helping her out of the cramped little car.

"No." As they drew near the roller coaster ticket booth, Jenny tensed. Each time the roller coaster roared down the track, the ground trembled beneath her feet. The screams of its passengers were like the cries of frightened birds.

"Why not? It's fun. You don't know until you try."

"I just can't do it. I'll turn to stone." She tried to make a joke of it. Steve could be so

21

insistent sometimes, and she was scared to death.

"Oh, come on. You're a killjoy, you know it?" Steve thrust his hands fiercely in his pockets.

"Steve, I just don't enjoy the roller coaster. It's not fun for me, so why should I go on it? I don't like being scared."

"That's why it's so much fun, dummy." He scowled at her, but she could tell he wasn't really mad.

"So go with somebody who thinks it's fun to be scared, then."

Exasperated, he threaded his arm through hers, dragging her to the next ride, the underground train. Jenny breathed a sigh of relief once they were inside the stifling cave, glad that at least she'd won that round with Steve.

As long as she didn't go on any scary rides, everything was great. But the minute anyone suggested the roller coaster or one of those other high-flying contraptions, Jenny absolutely froze. Once, she'd gone on the Matterhorn bobsleds at Disneyland, thinking they were slow, leisurely little cars, and when they started whipping around and through that mountain, she had been gripped with fear. Her family never forced her to try anything faster than the merry-go-round, and Jenny was determined not to be talked into it by anyone else.

Brooke, on the other hand, was more like Steve, loving the thrill of a ride that sent stomachs up into throats and heads spinning into dizziness. Jenny realized, with regret, that she wasn't really the most exciting person to bring to an amusement park, and she was torn all night long between her fear and wanting to please Steve.

"Can you handle the ferris wheel?"

"I—I don't know. I don't really like it, you know."

"Oh, come on. It doesn't go fast. We can't just ride the kiddie rides." Steve bought two tickets before she could protest further.

"Aren't you enjoying yourself?" he asked while the ferris wheel dipped sharply downward, sending the night rushing past Jenny's ears. The ocean, beach and lights blurred into a great blob. She held on tight to the metal bar in front of her, and through clenched teeth muttered, "It's okay."

Steve laughed at her, dropping his arm casually about her shoulders, but even his warmth couldn't dispel her terror. Only after they were off the ride could she breathe normally again.

"My suggestion this time. How about the merry-go-round?" Jenny ventured.

"Kiddie stuff," scoffed Steve, clamping his visor down over his hair. Jenny wondered why he wore that hat at night, when there was no sun to keep out of his eyes.

"Okay, I'll ride it. Let's see who can collect the most rings."

Jenny was pretty good at reaching from her saddle, getting the timing right so that she could hook a finger around one of the rings just as it popped into the mechanical hand. She salvaged six rings to Steve's three.

"Hey, we've found something you're good at. No offense." Steve laughed. "Let's see how you do with the balloon throw."

Jenny wasn't much good with balloons, but she did win a small china ashtray. She gave it to Steve for his mom because no one in her family smoked. Then Steve tried his hand at the shooting gallery.

"Where'd you learn to shoot like that?" Jenny asked him, impressed by his skill.

"My dad used to take me hunting when he lived with us. I've brought down a couple of bucks in my time," he announced proudly. "We used to drive to Idaho every October with a couple of his buddies. Great fun—camping out, tramping around in the woods all day. Loved it."

"I thought you were a solid surfer," Jenny teased him.

"No, only three-quarters."

Whap! went the gun, giving Steve enough points to choose a large prize.

"Here." He handed the tokens to Jenny. "Choose one of those animals up there."

"You're kidding? I never believed people could win those things!"

"Sure they can. One of them just did. How about the Miss Piggy? Isn't she adorable? I'd fall for her if I hadn't met you first."

She elbowed him. "Oh, come on. You want me to choose?"

"Well, yeah." He looked amused. "What am I gonna do with a stuffed animal?"

"You've got a point." Jenny beamed at Steve, knowing the choice she should make— to make him happy. There was a smaller stuffed bear which looked cuddlier than the conceited Miss Piggy, but, after all, Steve had won the prize. "I'll take Miss Piggy," she decided aloud.

"America's sweetheart," the cigar-smoking attendant quipped, handing over the pig in her frilly pink dress.

"Thanks, Steve." Jenny's eyes shone with gratitude as she hugged the pig to her chest.

"No big deal. I had fun winning it," he said.

They ate cotton candy and sampled the corn dogs at Joe Eliot's stand, a friend of Steve's. The two boys joked around and Jenny listened, quietly munching on her corn dog, not having anything to add to the conversation about surfing. Honestly, sometimes she thought she ought to learn how to surf just so she could join in. But then, Steve probably felt slightly left out when she got together with her friends to gab.

"I put two skegs on my board. You'll have to see it," Steve was saying.

Joe, who had a build like a gorilla, seemed really impressed. "Yeah? Sounds good. Been thinking of redoing my old one."

"Did you see Farrell's new board?"

"Not yet. Heard it's good, though."

Finally, the boys finished talking. Jenny

25

and Steve walked along the beach for a while. The colored lights from the Boardwalk made bright, thin ribbons upon the black face of the water, and Jenny loved the quiet slap of the gentle waves against the shore.

Walking along the beach with a surfer was not like walking with an ordinary person, Jenny knew from experience. While she enjoyed its beauty, Steve was checking out the possibility of tomorrow's surf—always in search of the perfect wave.

So she was happily surprised when Steve's arm stole around her waist and he drew her to him, kissing her fully on the mouth. Jenny wrapped her arms around his neck, and kissed him back, little thrills coursing through her.

She closed her eyes, drinking in Steve's closeness, the salt wind and the crisp, clear night, wanting to memorize it—and wishing they could be like that forever.

2

Remember Brian Halsey?" Shelly shoved a painted comb into her unruly hair.

"Oh, yeah. What about him?" Jenny feigned casualness. She had thought about Brian a lot during the week, figuring by now he'd be hobbling around on crutches.

"He's got to have an operation, poor guy. Smashed some bones in his leg. It's not a simple break like they thought."

"Really? Oh, no. That sounds terrible," Jenny blurted out in spite of herself. "I didn't think he'd be in hospital very long. Didn't he seem up to you?"

"Sure. But that's an act. You know how guys are. Always have to make you think they're really tough," Shelly replied knowingly, smoothing her rust-brown cords. "I wish I could lose about ten pounds. Then these pants would fit really well."

"They look nice, Shelly," Jenny reassured her, but it was true she could stand to lose a few pounds. The fabric stretched into tight wrinkles across her abdomen, even after she sucked in her waistline.

"I told you, just looking at food makes me fat. You think people have it made," lamented Shelly, dropping a crocheted poncho over the whole ensemble.

"Jay will think you look great." Jenny smiled and put the finishing touches on her friend's hair. She was meeting Jay downtown.

Shelly left, a little out of sorts. It's funny, Jenny thought, how when one thing isn't quite right about yourself, it can spoil your whole day. She hoped that wasn't going to happen to Shelly.

Skip called and asked Jenny to the birthday party they were throwing for Mr. Rice at the hospital. He was sixty-four today—a patient who had broken an ankle riding on his grandson's skateboard. "It'd be great if you could come," Skip urged. "You're one of his favorites."

Having no plans, Jenny agreed to go. Mr. Rice was one of her favorites, too.

Delia Whitney, the head nurse, had ordered a big cake for Mr. Rice. Jenny and Skip volunteered to bring it up from the cafeteria, stopping at the gift shop on their way. Mr. Rice liked scarves, so Jenny bought one and had it gift wrapped.

Mr. Rice was ecstatic over the birthday surprise, and made a big fuss over the enormous sheet cake. "Save some for my grandkids, now. Rolie feels so guilty about my being in here, on account of it's his skateboard. But I told him, next we're going hang gliding, so watch out!"

"You're going to be a regular customer, Mr. Rice," Jenny teased. She cut a second piece of cake to take down to Brian Halsey.

"What a surprise!" Brian's face lit up when he saw Jenny enter the room. "You were there when I was admitted, right?"

"Uh, yes." Jenny held out the piece of cake. "I thought you might like some birthday cake. One of the patients, Mr. Rice, turned sixty-four today."

"You came down here for a patient's birthday?" Brian asked.

"Well, yeah. He's one of my favorite people." She explained how he broke his ankle. Brian laughed. "So how're you doing?"

"Okay. But they're operating on my leg. It got more smashed than they thought. Have to wait till Monday to get my operation, you know. All the doctors are playing golf over the weekend. Oh, sorry." He blushed. "Didn't someone tell me your dad was a doctor?"

"Doesn't matter." She giggled. "My dad doesn't play golf, anyway."

"A noncomformist, huh?" He laughed softly, blue eyes dancing. "Good cake. It's not from the hospital kitchen, is it?"

"No, a local bakery."

"Are you interested in medicine as a career?" he asked.

"I want to be a doctor," she replied. "How about you?"

"I want to be a veterinarian. Right now, I raise all kinds of animals—hamsters, cats, dogs, mice, goldfish, parrots. I raise Siamese kittens, too. At least I know this won't interfere with that part of my future." He glanced at his sheet-shrouded legs, a look of regret clouding his features.

"What do you mean? You'll get better. This isn't a forever thing," she consoled him.

"Well, I might not be able to run track anymore after this. I'm pretty banged up." His eyes held hers.

"I'm sure . . ." Jenny's throat closed over the words. How could she be sure? She couldn't tell him some consoling words that didn't fit—that were just lies—could she? That wasn't right, for she really didn't know his situation at all. "Things'll work out," she said finally.

"Yeah. I like running, but it's a good thing I've got other interests, right?" He grinned, his blue gaze penetrating her own so fiercely she quickly dropped her eyes.

"It's always good to have other interests," she agreed softly.

"Right. So what are you into?" He smoothed the crisp sheet.

"Nothing special—the beach, and books."

Brian gazed at her pensively. The sun hitting her cheek suddenly felt too hot. "What're your interests?" It was a question she asked of many patients.

"I told you all of them, I think. Oh, except for pretty girls. They rate high on my list." He winked at her, a teasing light in his eyes. . . .

What am I doing here? Jenny asked herself. It's like I'm . . . flirting with this guy I hardly know, and I'm supposed to be Steve's girlfriend!

Abruptly, Jenny stood up, and glanced at her watch. "I just wanted to bring you the cake, so I'd better go now. See you."

"When?"

"I guess Friday. That's when I work."

"I'm scheduled for surgery tomorrow morning." Brian cocked his head to one side. The filtered sunlight caught the burnished sheen of his hair.

"Oh, well, good luck," Jenny said, annoyed to feel herself blushing. She closed the door quickly behind her, and began walking briskly down the hall.

"Where've you been?" Skip caught up with Jenny, squeezing her arm. "I've been looking all over for you since the party."

"I went to see another patient," she explained.

"You should see Rice. He's got your scarf draped around his neck and won't take it off." He chuckled.

They walked along the corridor which was

painted a pleasing combination of yellow and orange. "He'll have to take a bath some day," she quipped.

"Going home?" Skip turned to Jenny.

"Uh, no, I'm going to stop by my dad's office first."

"Well, see you Friday," Skip said. He sounded disappointed.

"Oh, who cares about stupid outcrops and bedding planes!" exclaimed Shelly, slamming down her geology book. "What good will all this do us fifty years from now, Jen?"

"It'll help us make exciting cocktail conversation," replied Jenny wryly. "I don't know— my dad says it helps you become a well-rounded person. If you only study what you like, that's all you'll know. I guess he has a point."

Science wasn't a problem for Jenny like it was for Shelly. She enjoyed the challenge and the absoluteness of science, whereas Shelly preferred history and social studies, with an eye on perhaps becoming a TV anchorperson when she got older.

"I figure I can pick up anything I don't know when I get to announce it on the six o'clock news," Shelly said. "I learn more from the news than I do at school already."

"Well, come on, let's get to work. This isn't going to be one of those tests I can take with my eyes closed." Jenny handed her friend the geology textbook. It had slid to the rose-printed carpet. "I'll ask you ten questions, then you ask me ten. What is rock cleavage?"

The Flemings' house was of a saltbox design with a flat, pebbled roof, overlooking Capitola Beach. From the living room where the two girls sat studying, there was a beautiful view of the ocean and the esplanade, a curved narrow street lined with quaint restaurants and artsy-craftsy shops. Beyond lay the rebuilt wharf, which had been partially destroyed by a storm several years previously.

The house was quiet after school, unlike Jenny's; Mrs. Fleming worked until five-thirty. Jenny loved to sit on the tufted blue window seat and stare out at the sea, now turned a sullen gray that matched the sky looming threateningly above the wharf— which from that distance resembled an arrangement of matchsticks.

Often, she and Steve sat there in the evenings while his mom made popcorn. They would steal kisses when Steve's mother wasn't looking, in between watching the twinkling ribbon of wharf lights around the bay.

Funny, just being in Steve's house when he wasn't home gave Jenny an uneasy feeling. She felt that he could walk in the door any moment and overhear their crazy conversations. He was out surfing as usual, but she was always careful about what she talked about at his house, not wanting him to catch her talking about him. That was one of the awkward things about dating your best friend's brother.

"Did Steve ask you to the prom?"

"Oh, no, he hasn't," replied Jenny. "Is he going to?"

"I don't know. I'm going to ask Jay." Shelly winked, her dimples deepening. "I hope he'll say yes."

"He probably will."

But Jenny wasn't really listening to Shelly— she was hoping Steve would take her to the prom.

Jenny had never been to a formal dance before, and she could just imagine how gorgeous Steve would look in a tux, with his beautiful tan and sun-streaked hair. And together—well, after she got a formal dress and fixed herself up—they could make a great couple.

"I'll tell you the truth, Jen. I've never seen Mr. Surf City"—Shelly used her affectionate nickname for her brother—"in a tux and it might take wild horses to stuff him into one," Shelly said. "Anyway, he doesn't confide in me, so any information I find out about him is strictly on the sly, get it?" She hunched over, shifty-eyed, and Jenny burst out laughing.

Most of the inside poop Shelly provided Jenny in regard to Steve's activities was trivial stuff Steve never guessed, because Shelly was as nosy as an anteater at sniffing out things. Plus, a lot of it was information a boy wouldn't think about concealing from anyone, such as what his favorite vegetable was, how his room was decorated and what his favorite movies were (surf and horror).

When Jenny first told Shelly she liked Steve, Shelly had supplied her with a heap of trivia to help her know Steve and his habits better— who his friends were, every ingredient of the health drink he fixed himself in the mornings, where he was at every hour of the day and all the girls he'd ever dated. It was very strange to know all this about a person when you really only knew him well enough to mutter "hi" once in awhile. Of course, Shelly thought it was just great. She wished she'd known half that much about the guys she dated.

But Shelly, in Jenny's opinion, was one of a kind. She was always doing things like phoning Jenny, then putting Steve on the line. An incurable busybody!

When they had finished studying, Shelly drove Jenny home. Jenny was still taking driver's training and had her permit, so she was able to drive with her parents, but she was pretty nervous about it. She marveled at how well Shelly handled a car, and wondered if she would ever learn. So far, she was only safe on quiet, isolated backroads.

Just as Shelly swung the car into the Carlsons' driveway, rain dotted the windshield. The house looked small under such a brooding sky.

Jenny hurried up the path. Inside, her mother was building a fire.

"Hi, honey."

"Hi. Wow, a fire looks great, Mom." Jenny peeled off her coat and knelt down to hold her palms over the tiny, spluttering flames. Then she broke up some kindling to sprinkle over the top.

The living room was full of comfortable, overstuffed chairs and antique marble-topped tables left by Jenny's grandmother. A golden glow from the fireplace now flickered over the room, giving everything a warm look.

Spurred by the atmosphere, Jenny made hot chocolate and she, Brooke and her mother sat in the living room watching the fire, listening to the pelting rain outside.

"Where's Steve?" asked Brooke.

"Surfing. Can you believe it, in this weather?" Jenny had a vision of him tumbling around in the restless surf, hardly aware of the rain until it fell in buckets.

"Maybe he's part fish," Brooke suggested, swinging her long legs over the side of a deep chair. "Connie thinks he's really cute. Ya better watch out, Jen!"

"Who—me or Steve?" Jenny sighed. "Connie Letterman thinks everyone's cute, Brooke."

"All my friends want boyfriends like yours when they get into high school," Brooke said.

"What about you?"

"I want one who likes to do everything I like to do," Brooke announced. "I don't care what he looks like."

"Steve and I like to do some of the same things," Jenny said carefully, but she knew it sounded defensive.

"Jenny, you really shouldn't tie yourself down," her mother advised. "It's stifling."

"Oh, Mom. What's wrong with having a steady boyfriend?" Jenny argued. Her mother had never said that she disapproved of Steve directly, but Jenny was aware of her feelings about him, nevertheless. Mom was always nice to him, but Jenny could tell that she was just being polite.

"You've got plenty of time to settle down with the same person. Why start so young?" Mrs. Carlson wanted to know.

"Who said anything about settling down? Didn't you ever have a steady boyfriend?" Jenny demanded, irritated by the whole subject.

"Not one in particular. I had lots of boyfriends, and I never got serious until I met your father. By then, I was much older," Mrs. Carlson explained.

"I don't think it works that way for me," Jenny decided aloud, annoyed with her mother for making an issue out of it. It wasn't her going with a boy that bugged Mom, it was Steve, and she knew it. He was a nice, well-mannered person, so why didn't Mom like him? It didn't make any sense.

Anyway, Jenny consoled herself, Dad never acted that way about Steve. Her father was always a little more easygoing than Mom, but if they'd both been reserved about her boyfriend, she really would have something to worry about.

"How's the young man who was in the accident?" Mom asked.

"Oh, Brian." Jenny guessed he would've

gotten out of surgery around eleven, and by now, midafternoon, he'd be coherent. "I was going to call and see how he's doing. He had surgery on his leg today."

"I spoke to Ellie Menkin today," her mother said, explaining about some meeting they had both attended.

Boy, news travels fast, Jenny thought, hoping her mother didn't detect the flush rising in her cheeks as she stepped into the hall to use the phone.

"Hey, Jenny. Am I glad to hear your voice." Brian sounded sleepy and labored, so Jenny guessed he must just be coming out from the effects of medication. "I'm sorta tired. Sorry I sound so weird. . . ."

"It's really okay. I understand. I know what it's like. I had some wisdom teeth pulled one time and it felt as though I were pulling myself out from under all these heavy layers of sleep."

"Exactly." He seemed relieved that she explained for him. "They say the operation was a success. I'll be good as new."

"That's wonderful, Brian." An overwhelming tide of relief swept over her.

"When do you come on duty? Friday night?"

He remembered her schedule. She smiled into the receiver. "Yes. I work for three hours, usually from seven to ten. I don't know where I'll be working this week."

"Try to stop by, okay?"

"You'll still be in the hospital?"

"Yeah. They might let me go Friday. I'll let you know."

"Okay."

"Hey, my mom's here. I'll call you. And Jenny?"

"Yeah?"

"You're going to make a great doctor. I can tell."

Those special words wrapped around Jenny like a pair of arms. She wanted so much to believe him.

"Thanks, Brian. We'll see," she replied, clamping down her excitement. "Take care of yourself."

"I will."

Jenny leaned back against the wall and closed her eyes. She imagined Brian's amused expression, overlaying a seriousness she guessed he rarely expressed. I hardly know him, she thought, and yet I can't get him out of my mind. . . .

3

Evan Cornell lived next door to Jenny. He was skinny as a beanstalk, freckled, loved classical music, and on a nice day when he cranked his windows wide open, strains of Mozart wafted across the lawns, along with Evan's deep baritone. Jenny and Evan were good friends, but Jenny hadn't seen him for six weeks, since he'd been in Mexico City on a student exchange program.

The night before she had heard his parents' Lincoln purr into the driveway, and she was anxious to talk to him about his trip. She walked along the pebbled walkway that joined their houses, finding Evan relaxing in the porch swing with a travel book.

"Hi, Jenny. Good to see you. How've you been?" He unfolded his long legs to give her a big hug.

"Hi, Evan. It's been a long time. I heard your car in the driveway last night and couldn't wait to come over. So how was it? Got your postcard of the ruins, by the way."

"It was fabulous! Fabulous ruins, fabulous food . . ." He rattled on and on. "It's a good thing the peso is devalued down there because I'm sure my spending money wouldn't have stretched that far. Most of us went crazy. Mr. Wiseman brought extra funds for those who overspent, like Eliza Berendt, who went crazy buying serapes, pastries and guitars for every member of her family. I'm surprised she was allowed on the plane to come home, she was so overloaded."

"How did you do otherwise? Did you lose anybody?" Jenny laughed at his description of Eliza, who was known to be a spendthrift.

"No. Not a soul, although I think Mr. Wiseman would've liked to lose Penny Taylor. When we were hiking around the ruins, she constantly whined about her sore feet. Everyone else was a trooper. Never complained. Enjoyed every minute of it."

"Even you?" Jenny teased. Evan was a guy for all seasons—he jogged a couple of miles per day, played piano, sang, was a star on the track team—so Jenny could easily imagine him trekking through the ruins.

"Even me." He frowned at her. "My Spanish has improved. Of course, I'm far from fluent, but I can understand it better."

Evan mashed his painter's cap down over

his ears and pushed his sunglasses higher onto his nose. "Oh, and the food—did you notice I put on a little weight?"

"Where? Between your ears?" Jenny honestly couldn't imagine a single ounce on that lean frame.

He socked her playfully in the forearm. "All those refritos and tortillas . . ."

"Yeah, I bet. Funny, they don't stick to your ribs, though."

"Let me just tell you my host family was very hospitable. Carlos, the son who's a year younger than me, is coming to stay with our family in a few weeks. He'll be attending school with me, too. It's a great program, Jenny."

"I'd like to go sometime," she responded wistfully.

"I went to school with Carlos. We had language classes in the morning, then history and math, then lunch, and our afternoons were virtually free, except on days when we had planned tours. Carlos and his friends showed me different parts of the city. We even went to a bullfight."

"Ugh. How gory."

"It's really not that bad."

"I suppose. Are you up to jogging down to the pond?" Jenny asked, anxious to change the subject.

"Give me a minute to get my gear."

He went inside, and Jenny played jacks with his little sister, Bebe. Jenny let her win, since she was only three and didn't know exactly what the game was all about, but was very happy to have an older person play with her.

Jenny and Evan jogged at about the same pace down the winding dirt path to the pond in back of Evan's house, which was surrounded by pines and dense shrubbery. Between breaths, Evan talked about his trip, then suddenly as they started downhill, he asked, "How're things going with Steve, Jen?"

"Oh, pretty good." Jenny wondered why Evan asked—he usually had very little to say to Steve. They weren't really friends, as their interests lay in very different areas. "Still surfing," she responded brightly. She stopped to tie her shoe.

"Steve still has the 'attitude,' Jen. Not like you." Evan ran ahead, ducking a low-hanging branch.

Jenny hurried to catch up. "What do you mean by that?"

"You're pretty much upbeat, and Steve's not—he's far from it."

"He has good qualities," she defended him, feeling prickly. "You just don't know him very well."

"Maybe," was all Evan would say in response. Then he hummed a bar of Bach's Brandenburg concerto.

Jenny hop-skipped and hummed along with him. When he got to the pond, turned around and caught sight of her funny gait as he came down the path, he started laughing.

"If only Bach could see you now!"

"He'd wonder what I was doing with his music." She giggled as she caught up to him. "What he didn't realize was that he wrote good jogging music."

"Time your heartrate while jogging to Bach," joked Evan. "He's ordered and precise. Won't set your heart jumping."

They sat on the damp grass and skipped stones into the pond. The glassy surface received them with a hearty plop, sending silver ripples toward its banks. Goldfish shimmered in the murky water when their scales momentarily caught the sunlight.

Evan turned to Jenny, the water's brilliance reflected in his eyes. She was aware that she'd never seen him look that way before. She'd been thinking of Steve, of how uneasy he made her feel sometimes, when Evan said softly, almost inaudibly, "You're really nice, Jenny. I like you."

"That's good, Evan." She laughed. "Since we have to live next door to each other, it pays to be on good terms. We've been friends a long time."

"Yeah, friends."

She shot him a sharp look. "What's that supposed to mean?"

He shrugged. "Oh, nothing." He glanced at his watch. "Let's head back. Mom was supposed to pull an angel food cake out of the oven right about now. Maybe, if we hurry, we can get a nice warm slice."

"Race ya?" Jenny challenged, which was silly because Evan always beat her by a mile.

"Sure. You're easy." He chuckled, jumping to his feet. They got in starting position. "Ready, set, go!"

"I'm going to the prom with Nat Helm," Doris Partlow said, shimmying into her gym clothes. She was petite and dark-haired, with large eyes cupped by jutting cheekbones.

"He asked you already?" Shelly was incredulous. "It's so early."

"Better early than never," Doris shot back gleefully.

"Hate to burst your bubble, but maybe he asked you early so he has a chance to change his mind," Millie Onslow offered wryly. "That happened to me last year. Don Winters invited me to go a month early, then he changed his mind two weeks later and wanted to take someone else."

"That's terrible!" Jenny was outraged.

"That's life, I'm afraid."

"Had you ever dated him before?" Jenny wanted to know.

"Once or twice. Then he started seeing Denise Roy, and he wanted out of the date." Millie sighed, sweeping a thick lock of auburn hair from her eyelashes. "It worked out okay, though. Damon Courtney, my next-door neighbor, took pity on me, and we went together. Had the best time."

"Well, that's not going to happen to me," Doris announced huffily. "Nat and I have been eyeing each other for months."

"That long?" Millie's eyebrows rose in twin arches of surprise.

Doris blushed. "Oh, stop it. Anyway, I can see your point," she babbled on. "David Collins is a really good friend of mine, and we've done a lot together, like going to dances. We always have fun. Sometimes boys as friends can be better than boyfriends," she offered sagely.

"Sometimes," agreed Millie. "And often, romance changes a friendship between girls and boys. It's hard to remain friends with a boy after you've broken up with him, for instance. I mean, there's something about romance that spoils friendship for awhile."

"Except, if you aren't friends with a guy first, how can you ever have a romance?" Shelly questioned. "Jay and I are good friends."

"You've just started a romance, that's why. I know it's hard to imagine, but if you break up, the friendship will get weird. Maybe after you're over each other, you can be friends again," Doris said.

Jenny laughed. "If we hang around you seniors for awhile, we'll get educated."

"And jaded." Shelly scowled. "You guys are cynics."

"You are listening to the voices of experience, Shelly," Millie said dramatically. "Get your heart broken a few times, shed some tears, you'll see what it's like."

It was common knowledge that Millie was currently getting over Eddie Marcus, so what she said had to be taken with a grain of salt. Nevertheless, Jenny couldn't help thinking about Steve and wondering about their relationship.

"Love sure is tough," grumbled Doris.

"I don't want to hear anymore!" cried Shelly, shaking her head violently. "Jenny, let's go play volleyball. These guys are not good for our health!"

They all laughed and raced each other out to the gym.

Jenny had a good strong serve, so she started off the game. The ball spiraled through the air, landing in the first row of the opposing team, who sent it into the net. The Royals, Jenny's team (or more rightfully Millie's, as she was team captain), squealed with excitement at their first point.

"Come on, Jen—give us another point!" Millie yelled. She was a large girl who was a formidable presence on the court.

Jenny served again, and this time the ball landed between two second-row players who did nothing, which sent the team captain into a rage. Jenny was smugly pleased that Millie was an encouragement rather than a big pain like Francine Whalen of the Stealers. Millie might have funny ideas about guys, but she was great on the volleyball court.

Francine Whalen was furious by the time Jenny had hit three points in a row. Finally, on the fourth serve, Ellie Terris of the Stealers sent the ball back over the net, starting a volley that ended with Millie fumbling the ball.

While they played, Jenny's thoughts wandered back over the locker room conversation about friendships with boys. Could she remain friends with Steve if they ever broke up? she wondered. Of course, the thought of breaking up was frightening enough, especially since she'd never been through that experience before. Other people's testimonies were scary to her, and she preferred not to even ponder it. Feelings were so fragile, and Jenny wondered how she would feel towards Steve after sharing a certain closeness, then having an argument, or just simply coming to a parting of ways, as she heard people put it.

Jenny scooted forward to the second row to slam the ball over the net. Francine fumbled it while yelling instructions to her team, thereby giving the Royals another point.

The Royals had difficulty containing their excitement. Francine glowered. A procession of boys filed through the gym. Jenny picked out Steve's self-assured swagger as he strode beneath the basketball hoop, and she waved. He waved back, then looked away from her. It amazed her how the boys enjoyed the stir they created amongst the girls, yet they behaved as though they didn't know they were the objects of such attention.

"You should just ignore them," Jenny told Doris, who blushed at the sight of Nat.

"How can I ignore him?" Doris sighed. "He looks so great in his gym shorts."

"All of them act ultra cool around us. We show how we feel about them. But if we didn't, they might wonder why, we might play a better game and they might react in some way," Jenny figured aloud.

"What're you saying, Jen?"

"She's this vast fountain of information," said Shelly.

"I just wonder what they would do if we just went on as if we didn't notice them. I mean, we don't act that way if girls file through here, do we?"

"No."

"So why do we get silly for them?"

"Good question, Jen. One I often asked myself." Millie nodded. Jenny guessed she could count on Millie for a fierce reaction. "This is the twentieth century, and why we are reduced to such dumbness for the sake of men is beyond me."

"Let's try an experiment," Jenny suggested, fired up by Millie's enthusiasm. "Tomorrow when they come through here, as they do every day after track—even more reason to not make a big deal about them—let's just go on as if we don't see them. The other team will probably act silly, but they'll wonder why we don't."

"It won't work," Shelly observed. "They'll still be getting the attention from them." She nodded in the direction of the Stealers, who would be replaced by another team the next day.

"Yes, but I bet they'll wonder why we don't give it to them," Jenny insisted.

Millie giggled. "All right, take your positions. Let's play ball."

The next day, Jenny didn't wave at Steve when he walked through the gym. Millie didn't wave at anyone, either, and Doris refrained from even glancing at Nat. Shelly didn't bat an eyelash, which was an amazing feat for Shelly. The boys looked somewhat perplexed, but sure enough, the other team, the Red Hens, captained by Maxine Grass, provided the attention they were accustomed to.

However, the Red Hens' obvious confusion worked in the Royals' favor—the Royals scored five points during the time the boys occupied the gym.

"You guys better pay attention to the ball or you're gonna lose this game," Millie warned, suppressing a grin.

Titters arose from the smitten Red Hens, who attempted to send the ball back, each player sending it spinning with no direction.

"Net ball! Our serve!" Shelly jumped up and down.

A roar of applause erupted from the boys, who had stopped to watch the game.

"Don't stop now, girls," Millie coached in a fierce whisper as the team huddled around her. "We've got their attention, but we're not giving one ounce to them, just to this game. Now keep your mind on this ball!"

"Good serve, Jenny!"

Jenny heard Steve's encouraging shout behind her, which sent excited tingles down her spine. Could she do it with him watching her every move?

"Come on, Jen." Millie's terse instructions helped her send the ball soaring. Fortunately, the other team was still suffering from butterfingers, and they lost it.

The Royals were getting very close to the fifteen points that would win them the game.

"Good one, Jenny!" Steve again.

"Yea, team!"

Nat—cheering for Doris. Doris was not good at hiding her pleasure. Her face turned beet red, but she managed to ignore him sufficiently enough to smash the ball down on the first-row opposition with a powerhouse punch, which earned another point and a round of applause.

The Red Hens, seeing their loss as imminent, seemed to give up. The Royals had fifteen points when the shower bell rang.

"We won!" Everyone squealed in ecstasy . . . everyone, that is, except the glum-faced Red Hens.

As they jogged out of the gym, Jenny smiled at Steve. He grinned back, shook a fist at her, obviously pleased at her victory. More importantly, she was pleased with herself and the team effort. She would've liked to have thrown her arms around him, but she wasn't about to do that after the deal she'd made with the girls. Besides, Millie was buying Cokes for everyone at the snack bar and she didn't want to miss out.

It suddenly occurred to Jenny that the Royals had only two more games to play—if they won, they could play for the championship.

4

Friday rolled around before Jenny was ready for it. The geology test had occupied her thoughts for most of the week, and she hadn't seen much of Steve. He called nearly every night to tease her about being such a drudge, which, although he was only kidding, bothered her.

School was really important to Jenny, especially her science classes. She had a long road of studying ahead of her if she planned to go into medicine, and she was glad that she'd established good study habits early. To Steve, school was a bore—something he had to do. He enjoyed sports, metal and wood shops, but admitted he never liked any of his science classes.

On Friday, Steve suggested picking Jenny up from the hospital and going back to his house to watch television. Jenny accepted eagerly, not having seen him all week, except at school. Also, she nursed the small hope that maybe he might ask her to the prom. In spite of Shelly's warning about Steve never going to proms, Jenny secretly thought that since this was his last year of high school, he might want to.

At school, posters showing a couple silhouetted against a black background announced "Midnight Lace." The morning bulletin ran daily announcements about tickets, and everyone was talking about it.

Roger Bouchet, with whom Jenny walked from Geology to Algebra every day, asked her if she was going to the dance. Figuring he was just making conversation, she told him no.

"Why are you asking, Roger? You usually don't get involved in school events, do you?" Jenny asked, curious. Roger was the studious type—sort of like herself—who had never shown an interest in dances before, to her knowledge.

Roger blushed, his dark eyes growing wide. "Well, uh, just asking, Jennifer." He stumbled over his words, and quickly said goodbye.

"Hey, wait a minute, Roger," Jenny called after him. "Is May going?" May Brown was his girlfriend, an owlish looking girl who actually looked a little like Roger.

"No, she doesn't dance. Besides, Jenny, May and I are just friends." Roger's blush deepened.

"Oh, I didn't know that." Jenny shot him a puzzled look, but said nothing. She was remembering the way May looked at Roger, as if the sun rose and set at his command.

Briefly, the thought crossed her mind that maybe Roger was interested in asking her to the dance. She hoped he wouldn't. Her heart was set on Steve asking her, and she didn't want to spoil that possibility, however slight, by accepting another invitation.

Jenny hastily changed the subject to the Algebra quiz they would be taking. Just then, Steve sauntered down the hall towards them.

"Hi, Jenny, Roger." Steve's gaze roamed over the two of them. "What class are you headed for?"

"Algebra," Jenny replied, suddenly feeling nervous under Steve's close scrutiny.

"Do you always walk to class together?" There was a twinge of sarcasm in Steve's tone, a crimping around the eyes.

"Yes, Steve. Didn't you know that? Roger's a good friend." She emphasized the word "friend" to be sure he didn't get the wrong idea.

"I'll be picking you up after work tonight, remember?" he said, as if confirming his hold on her.

"I remember. See you then." Jenny squeezed his hand affectionately, but he drew away, mumbled goodbye and disappeared down the hall.

"Mrs. Gandowsky tried to rip off some sheets," Skip whispered in Jenny's ear so that passing patients couldn't hear. "I saw a big

55

white lump sticking out of her suitcase, and she was trying to sit on the top to make it close. So I went in to help her. You should've seen her face!" He collapsed on a plastic chair, laughing.

"What did you say to her?" Jenny giggled. The picture of plump, henna-haired Mrs. Gandowsky sitting on her suitcase was almost too much to bear.

"I said . . ." Poor Skip had to take a deep breath. "'What do you think this is? The Sheraton Hotel? We don't give out free ashtrays and soap.' And she said she thought the hospital wanted people to take things—free advertising, you know. So I reminded her our sheets aren't even monogrammed."

"Crazy." Jenny shook her head in disbelief. "I guess some people figure they're paying hotel rates, why not get the same advantages."

"Come on, you two." Jackie Edwards, a pretty, brunette nurse, whistled into the nurses' station and, seeing a patient's light go on, breezed on out again. "Jenny, there's a prescription I want you to pick up. Skip, come with me."

Skip shrugged and followed Jackie.

The evening went by very quickly—Jenny picked up the prescription, changed bedding delivered a package, then wheeled a cartful of magazines and books around to the patients.

Mrs. Durant, an elderly woman in Room 302, had broken her hip falling down her front steps. Next to her bed she kept an impressive stack of movie magazines and romance novels.

"Have you got anything like this for me to read, love? Barbara Cartland is my favorite." She smiled, holding up a copy of one of the author's books in her arthritic, gnarled fingers.

Jenny was quite familiar with the books in her cart, mostly bestsellers, light reading and a few how-to's. "Here's one," she said, pulling out a slim volume.

"I've finished all these." Mrs. Durant pointed to her towering stack. "Can you pass them on to other patients?"

"Sure." Jenny took an armful of the novels and dumped them on the bottom of her cart, to be sorted later.

"Doesn't Mrs. Durant look a little like Barbara Cartland?" Shelly remarked later in the hall. She giggled. "All those frilly nightgowns she wears, and all that makeup. You'd think she was the queen or something."

"She enjoys herself." Jenny defended Mrs. Durant. "At least she's not afraid to be what she wants to be."

Jenny peeked into Brian's room and saw him laughing with a tall, slim girl with light brown hair. Who was she? His girlfriend? Jenny wondered. Later, she walked by and the girl was gone, so she went in.

"Jenny, good to see you." Brian waved, then punched his pillows into place to sit up. "Are all the pillows here this flat?"

"Sorry. Everyone complains about them, but there're no other kinds. Just use more."

"It's okay. They don't seem so bad . . . now that you're here." He grinned, eyes sparkling with pleasure.

Although she knew it was none of her business, she wondered what he'd talked about with the pretty girl who had just visited him. "I hope you're not getting too bored," she said. "I've got books and magazines outside."

He pointed to the tumble of books by his bedside. "I can learn a lot just lying here. Mom brought me some of my animal husbandry books."

"How long will you be in?"

"Who knows? You see, my lower leg, the fibula, was broken in four places. Maybe you know something about this."

"Not much," Jenny confessed. "My dad, being in pediatrics, gets a few broken bones. Go on. I'm all ears."

"So they wired together the pieces and I'll have to have surgery again to have the pins taken out. They say I'm in real good shape, so everything will be okay." The seriousness fell away, quickly replaced by amusement. "But one good thing about this is I get to enjoy remote-control TV."

Jenny laughed. "Keep me posted on your progress—and the afternoon movies."

Brian grinned. "What kind of doctor do you want to be, Jenny?"

"I'm not sure yet. I'll decide once I'm in med

school." She scooted the orange plastic chair away from the bed.

"Did you always want to be a doctor?"

"Well, yeah. Since I was a little girl. I used to bandage up my dolls and stuffed animals. Play hospital, you know. I nursed a sick bird back to health once, with my father's help. We found a little swallow that had fallen from its nest, and I spoke to pet shop owners and naturalists, and learned that it had to be fed with an eyedropper. It grew so big that eventually we had to let it loose, which was sad, because my family had grown very accustomed to it. But it squawked very loudly, and woke us up a lot, demanding to be fed."

Brian laughed. "Sounds like true dedication on your part."

"I think it must have been. I don't really remember when I turned my attention to nursing people. But I'm sure my parents' influence had something to do with it. I get a real sense of doing something worthwhile when I'm working around here, even if my jobs are pretty menial. It's still fun, and I get to talk to many different types of people."

"That's one advantage of being a medical doctor. You meet lots of different types of pets in veterinary medicine—some you'd rather not meet." Brian's eyes danced.

"Like boa constrictors?" Jenny laughed. "I meet some I'd rather not meet, too, believe me." She related the story of Mr. Sardoni who used to yank his IVs out and jump out of bed, scaring the nurses out of the room. He made it nearly impossible for doctors to treat him, and they released him early because he disturbed the other patients.

"One advantage about animals is that you can sedate them if they get out of control," Brian observed. "You're probably not allowed to knock someone out for their entire hospital stay."

"No." Jenny sighed, settling into her seat. "I think I'd like to specialize in pediatrics, like my father. What about you? Are there different areas of specialization?"

"Oh, you can specialize in large or small animals, or do both. There are farm and city practices, and nowadays, people are getting into the old house-call medicine. That's better for the animals who are too nervous to be moved. I'm interested in that right now."

Then Brian talked animatedly about track, and what a bummer it was that he wouldn't be going back to it for a long time, but he didn't dwell on the negatives. He seemed to avoid feeling sorry for himself. Jenny thought it was wonderful to have such a great attitude. It must be hard for an active person like Brian to be injured and bedridden for such a long time.

It was ten o'clock and time to go. Shelly would soon come looking for her.

"Enjoy TV," she told Brian. "And don't get square eyes."

When she left he was laughing.

* * *

Lost in her own thoughts, Shelly didn't notice Jenny's crazy expression as they headed for the parking lot where Steve waited.

"Jay's taking me to the dance!" Shelly bounded up and down like a little kid. "Can you believe it? I called him while I was on duty."

"Wow! I knew he'd go," Jenny responded, watching Steve comb his hair in the rearview mirror.

"Oh, wow! What am I going to wear?" Shelly was already mentally picking through her wardrobe.

"Wear for what?" grumbled Steve.

"To the *prom*, Steve. I'm going to the prom with Jay Sheldon," his sister called to him smugly, dangling her hair ribbon out the window. "Isn't that fantastic?"

"Earthshaking," Steve muttered sarcastically, grinning at Jenny. "Isn't it?"

Jenny's heart thudded so loudly she thought for sure he could hear it. Of course, she knew Steve wouldn't ask her to the dance in front of Shelly, but maybe when they got back to his house and everyone was busy, the opportunity would come up. . . .

But there was a houseful at the Flemings. Steve's mom, Nora, had brought home two coworkers and they occupied the living room. Rodney and Alexandra sat on the window seat—right where Jenny and Steve usually sat.

Nora insisted that Steve, Jenny and Shelly join them for a while—which ended up to be the rest of the evening. Shelly dropped out to make popcorn, but the group didn't break up until sometime after Jenny and Steve left to get her home before her curfew.

They talked about Rodney and Alexandra Leach nearly all the way to Jenny's house, even though Jenny's thoughts were somewhere else. She kept imagining Steve, very casually cutting in with, "Hey, do you wanna go to the prom with me, Jen?"

It would be so easy, natural. They knew each other well enough that he didn't have to get embarrassed about it, anymore than he'd get embarrassed asking her out on a regular date. Didn't he realize she couldn't ask *him*—it was up to him?

Her first prom. She could just visualize the kind of dress she would pick out—something sleek and satiny, pink or blue, which looked good with her hair.

"Hey, Jenny, are you there? How'd that Geology test go?" Steve placed his hand over hers and squeezed it affectionately, bringing her back to earth.

"Oh, uh, I think I did okay. Shelly and I studied most of the week. It's an interesting subject. I just have trouble remembering everything."

"Never took the class myself. You know me, always take the easy stuff."

"Come on, Steve. Stop putting yourself down." Jenny didn't like how he did that. It always made her feel too smart and serious.

"I'm not," he defended himself, the Toyota crunching noisily across the gravel in front of Jenny's house. "Ask me about surfing. I'm good at that. Or kissing. I do that well, too."

His lips found hers easily, and Jenny stroked the fine longish hair that grazed his collar, letting herself ride on the tide of sensations, feeling that she loved him so much she didn't know what to do with it all.

The porch light popped on suddenly and Jenny pulled away, not anxious to have her parents discover them making out.

"I'd better get inside." She smiled at him, motioning toward the door. "My folks."

"Oh, yeah. Their signal." Steve laughed. "Parents think they're so cool, don't they?"

"Yeah," she agreed, feeling warm all over as she skipped up to the front door.

"Jenny! Mail for you!"

Jenny rolled over to face the clock-radio on her bedside table. Ten o'clock. Not necessarily too early, but she loved to sleep late on a Saturday morning. On the other hand, her mom liked to have everyone up early on weekend mornings so she could get on with gardening or whatever she had planned.

When she became a doctor, Jenny figured she'd have to be available at all hours, so why not take advantage of it now?

Groaning, she stepped out of bed and

shrugged into her blue velour robe. The mail was on the kitchen table. The letter addressed to Jenny was actually a short note, written in an unfamiliar hand.

It read:

Jenny, you really are a sweet girl, and I love to be with you. Signed, Your Secret Admirer.

She couldn't stop smiling. The idea teased and delighted her. *Steve—dear Steve, it must be*—even though it didn't look like his usual handwriting. Maybe he'd gotten a friend to write the note for him. Nobody else would send her such a note, would they?

Dialing his number, Jenny was bubbling with excitement. "Hi, Steve? Yeah, I know it's early, but I wanted to thank you for your sweet note. I just know it's you."

"What note? I didn't send any note." He sounded sort of irritable, as though she'd roused him out of bed.

"You didn't send me a note signed, Your Secret Admirer? Oh, come on, who else would do that?"

"It wasn't me, Jen, I swear. Why would I do a dumb thing like that?" he insisted. "Must be one of your other boyfriends."

"Oh, yeah, sure. I'm surrounded by admirers." Her excitement evaporated into curiosity.

If Steve hadn't sent the note, who had?

* * *

"It's not my brother's handwriting, but that doesn't mean anything," Shelly said when she saw the note. "He could've had Ralph or one of his other friends write it for him. But it's definitely a boy's handwriting. See how cramped up and sloppily it's written."

"No kidding, Nancy Drew!" Jenny giggled.

"Hey, what about Roger Bouchet? You walk to class with him every day, don't you?" Shelly's eyebrows jerked up and down as if controlled by invisible strings.

"Well, yeah, but that's nothing. We're old friends and we have Geology and Algebra together," she said. Roger was nice, and Jenny had known him since kindergarten, but there certainly wasn't any romance between them. "I still think it's Steve," she said.

"Me, too," Jenny agreed.

All day, Jenny dreamed about Steve's secret thoughts—those special things he never told her—like how much he cared about her, how maybe he even *loved* her! Maybe that was taking it a little far, but then if he could write that kind of a letter, what more was he feeling for her? But why was he so shy about showing it?

After Geology, Roger fell into step beside Jenny, as he always did. "How'd you do on that test, Jen? Your usual A?" He grinned, making a wealth of freckles merge on his round, friendly face.

"Yes." Jenny blushed, feeling sort of embarrassed about her good grade, even though she'd studied awfully hard to get it. Of course, Roger was an A student, too, but she didn't want to seem boastful even to him.

"Good for you. Me, too. Cunningham's a real nerd sometimes, though. He really makes you struggle. Methinks he wrote some of those questions backwards." Roger liked to talk like Shakespeare, which earned him lots of laughs from other kids. He wore an English driving cap clamped down over his wild auburn curls, which he only removed in the classroom at the teacher's insistence. Everybody at school thought of Roger as "the guy with the hat."

Jenny laughed. Mr. Cunningham was known to try and trick students by rephrasing the test questions so that they didn't match those in the textbook.

"Hey, Jenny." Roger's voice dropped conspiratorially low. "I've been meaning to ask you . . . uh, are you going with Steve Fleming? I see you with him a lot. . . ."

"Well, yeah, sort of . . ." Jenny flushed bright pink. Steve had never said "We're going together" or "You're my girl" or anything definite, so she felt weird saying that they were going together. "But not really."

"You see a lot of each other, though. Right?" Roger pulled nervously at the brim of his cap.

"Sure." What was this leading up to?

"I was wondering if you ever dated anyone else, like to take in a movie or something."

"I—I never have, Roger, since Steve and I . . . we have a sort of unspoken agreement,

66

you know?" That sounded awfully vague, too, she realized, but she didn't know what to tell him, and she didn't want to hurt his feelings in any way.

"If you ever decide to, would you let me know?" Roger's smile came out stiff and cardboardy, and she smiled back.

"Sure, Roger."

Hastily, he scurried into Algebra before she could utter another word.

Maybe, Jenny considered, scooting to her desk, maybe Roger is my Secret Admirer?

"Hey, Jen! You want a ride home, or are you waiting for your Secret Admirer?" Steve asked sarcastically. He leaned an arm above her locker, gazing down at her as she spun the lock. A blond lock of his hair fell across the darker part and Jenny reached up to move it into place.

"That's not fair, Steve. For all I know, you're my Secret Admirer," she retorted, not mentioning Roger Bouchet.

"All this attention is gonna go to your head! You really think I'd send a stupid note like that?"

He relieved her of her pile of books, hoisted them under his arm and they left the building together, with Shelly walking behind them.

"Steve, you've got no class, you nerd," Shelly reprimanded him, catching up. "Any guy who sends a girl a letter like that is a real peach in my book."

"Now listen to who has no class," Steve

shot back. "If you could only find out who sent it, Shelly, maybe you could get him to send you one, too."

Jenny didn't say much, but she kept glancing at Steve all the way home. His handsome profile still excited her. She admired his deep tan against a white T-shirt, his sun visor pushed casually over the streaked hair.

But she was slightly hurt by his attitude about the note. If he thought the note was stupid, then he hadn't sent it, right? Well, maybe he did, and he wanted her to think it was some prankster. Or maybe he didn't want her to make such a big deal out of it.

Steve let Shelly out at their house, and then drove Jenny home.

"I don't appreciate you saying those things in front of Shelly," Jenny told him, breaking the silence between them. "I don't like your attitude about this whole thing. I don't think the note is stupid. Whoever sent it is sweet." She felt her heart pounding wildly in her chest, in anticipaton of his answer.

"Yeah, maybe he is." He hammered the steering wheel in frustration. "Look, I don't know what you're doing. I don't even know how you feel about seeing other guys . . ."

She cut him off quickly. "But we agreed we weren't going to date other people, didn't we?"

"Yes, but this makes me wonder if you're seeing someone else. Maybe Roger." Steve studied her closely.

"That's crazy!" Jenny was indignant. "Roger is my friend, and that's all. It's not fair of you to make that kind of assumption, and it bugs me that you don't trust me."

"I do trust you, Jenny, it's just . . ."

Jenny sensed there was more to his probing than met the eye. He made her angry, but she couldn't help but feel flattered that he feared she was too popular. But maybe he was just acting that way, to throw her off his trail. Still, his reaction unsettled her and made her a little nervous of just having friends like Roger. What would she tell Roger? Sorry, I can't walk to class with you anymore, my boyfriend doesn't like it?

No, Jenny refused to do that. Steve could be upset if he wanted to be, but she couldn't disrupt her friendships for him.

Finally, he broke the silence between them. "Hey, listen, Jenny. What I said about the note . . . I guess I'm just sore, that's all. I didn't do well on my English exam today."

"Sorry to hear that," Jenny answered. That explained a lot. Steve always felt insecure about his grades—especially English—and it didn't help matters any that Jenny was pretty good at the subject.

"Look, why don't we go to a movie tonight? Would you like that?"

When he leaned over to kiss her gently on the mouth, his visor pushed her hair out of place. She wanted to fix it, but didn't want to spoil the moment.

Yet, as quickly as her spirits had risen, they sank. "I can't go out tonight, Steve. It's a school night. Remember?"

He looked disappointed. "Oh, yeah. Well, take a raincheck. We'll definitely go on the weekend, okay?"

"Okay."

The weekend. They kissed once more before Jenny got out of the car and he drove off.

Jenny felt like a yo-yo, bounced up and down with Steve holding the string. She wondered if he was even aware of it. He hadn't asked her to the prom. Maybe he was working up to it, she hoped.

5

How's this one?" Shelly whirled from one dress rack to another, clutching an armful of formals while whipping more off the racks. "Or this?" She held a dreamy cream satin up to her waist.

Jenny couldn't resist the urge to touch it. The cool, slippery fabric slid between her fingers like rushing water. An overwhelming wave of envy flooded her. If only *I* were going to the prom, she thought.

"It's beautiful," Jenny replied enthusiastically, careful not to let Shelly know how she felt. "Try it on. I think it'll look good on you."

The two girls went into a dressing room. Dutifully, Jenny sat through Shelly's changes, offering comments where needed.

The cream satin was perfect, but Shelly wanted to try all the others, just to be sure she'd gotten the right one.

When she came to a red dress with layered ruffles, Jenny burst into giggles. "You can wear that on *The Gong Show*."

"Not to the prom? Aren't I super?" She spun around so that the dress formed a tent. It was the sort of style that would put fifteen pounds on Shelly's figure. "Honestly, someone will turn up in this thing, watch and see."

"Just as long as it isn't you."

"Why don't you try one on, Jen. Just for fun. Come on," Shelly urged, peeling off the red dress.

"No. What's the point?" Jenny rejected the idea, a lump forming in her throat.

"My brother better ask you to this dance, I swear," Shelly grumbled. "He doesn't know what he's missing. He's never been to a formal and this is his last chance."

"Don't say anything to him, Shelly. Promise?" Jenny entreated. The last thing she wanted was for Steve to feel sorry for her, or to think she had encouraged Shelly to bug him about the prom.

"Lighten up, will you? I'm not totally stupid, you know. I'll buy this dress, okay?" She gazed lovingly at the cream satin. "You really think it looks good?"

"Beautiful. It makes you look . . . like a princess." Jenny smiled at her.

The dress really did wonders for Shelly's figure; she looked slim and petite. It brought out her best feature—her catlike green eyes.

There was a soft, shimmery blue gown that

Jenny lingered over while Shelly paid for hers, imagining how she'd look to Steve in it. But that was all it was, she reminded herself glumly, just a dream. Steve wouldn't ask her. Her mom had said once that there were some people who were just too self-conscious to go to a dance like that, and get all dressed up. They were more comfortable in sweatshirts and jeans. Maybe Steve was one of them.

The two girls breezed down to the shoe department and Shelly tried on a multitude of shoes. Finally, she chose a pair of gold sandals with thin straps that looked perfect with the dress.

"What about jewelry? I don't have any!" Shelly wailed as they passed the jewelry counter. There were some cloisonné medallions on silken strings which caught her eye. She just had to have a gold one to match the dress and shoes.

"Are you through yet?" Jenny asked, pretending to faint from exhaustion. "If we don't get out of here, your mother's charge account is going to be in trouble."

Shelly laughed and flourished her new necklace as if she were some kind of movie star. "Oh, you know Mom. She'll scream for a few minutes and then she'll get all jazzed about the nice things I bought, and she'll calm down."

Jenny helped carry the packages out of the store. Sure, she'd dreamed of going to a prom before, but there was nothing like a shopping spree to make her long to go. Beside Shelly's triumphant, golden glow, it was hard not to feel jealous and wistful.

They piled Shelly's purchases in the trunk of the car, stopped for an ice cream, then drove to her house.

Jenny's heart stopped in her throat at the sight of Steve sprawled next to his motorcycle in the driveway.

"Look who's here," Shelly said, driving the car up within inches of Steve's ratty sneakers.

He raised his head and blinked at the two girls, obviously preoccupied with the motorcycle's problems, then opened a blackened palm in greeting.

"Where did you two go?"

"Spending money. Want to see my new prom dress? It's beautiful." Shelly pulled it carefully from its tissue wrapping paper and clutched it to her waist, then spun around the driveway.

"The neighbors'll think you're loony. Put that thing away." Steve shook his head and turned back to his greasy parts.

"Kick him for me, will you, Jenny?"

Jenny smiled, not wanting to get involved in their brother-sister argument. Shelly folded the dress and put it away, talking the whole time.

"I'm so excited I can't believe it. The dance is going to be so great."

Jenny knelt down next to Steve to see what he was doing—not that she understood anything about the mechanics of the bike. "What's wrong with it, Steve?"

"Oh, the clutch is messed up, I think," he mumbled, not looking up. "I don't have the money to get it fixed until next week."

There were smudgy grease streaks in the light part of his hair, and a smear of oil on his cheek.

"You have to be a doctor to figure this out," Jenny said, marveling at Steve's ability to know one thing from another on the machine.

"Yeah."

"You ought to take Jenny to the prom, Steve. I mean, here you are a senior, and you've never been to a prom before." Shelly beamed innocently over her mountain of packages.

Jenny shot her a murderous look. "Shelly . . ."

"No, really." She didn't stop even though Steve was blushing a near purple. "Why don't you take her? If you don't, somebody else might." Shelly winked at Jenny, who scowled back, her face growing hot.

Jenny closed her eyes in disbelief. *I always knew Shelly had a big mouth, but this is too much. . . .*

"Bug *off*, will ya, Shelly?" Steve growled, his face dark with anger. Avoiding Jenny's eyes, he stuck the visor on backwards, so that the green brim grazed his shoulder blades and turned the ratty sweatshirt he wore a slimy green color.

Shelly sailed into the house with her bundles. Jenny stood, rooted to the cement, wondering what to say or do.

"See you, Steve," she said woodenly, starting up the path. She couldn't even bring herself to say she was sorry for what Shelly did.

"Hey, wait." Steve straightened, smoothing his hair back with the inside of his arm. His eyes searched hers. "Do you really wanna go to that prom? I didn't know. . . ."

"No . . . it's all right, Steve, really," she heard herself mumbling. It was as though she were listening to some other girl fumble around for an explanation instead of herself. "I know you . . . I don't want to go just because Shelly—"

"No." He cut her off, but he looked uncomfortable, as though he'd been squeezed into clothing that didn't fit. "I mean, I just never thought of it. I don't like to dance, so it wouldn't be any fun."

"It's okay, Steve, really. It was dumb of Shelly to bring it up," Jenny said, her voice thin and reedy, ready to break. She wanted to flee. "I'll see you later."

Quickly, she went inside, making a beeline for Shelly's bedroom.

Naturally, Steve was angry. Who wouldn't be, put on the spot like that? Man, she could just *strangle* Shelly. Didn't she realize she couldn't run other people's lives?

Shelly was standing in front of the oblong vanity mirror, a dreamy expression on her face as she tried on the new necklace.

That made Jenny even more furious.

"Somebody ought to put a lock on your mouth," she announced.

Shelly blinked at her in surprise, lowering the poised necklace as if it obstructed her view.

"Oh, yeah? Well, if somebody doesn't say something, you and old loverboy out there would never get anywhere," she returned hotly.

"Which would be a whole lot better than having your kind of help, thank you very much."

Jenny spun around and left, bidding Steve a hasty farewell as she passed. She broke into a run down the steep hill to the bus stop.

"What's gonna happen to me?" Six-year-old Jamie Saunders studied Jenny with round, fearful blue eyes, expecting the very worst.

Jenny was escorting him to X-ray. She reached for his hand, which he offered willingly. "Well, they're going to take a picture of your insides to see if you cracked a rib when you fell down the stairs. It doesn't hurt a bit."

"Ha-ha. That's what the nurse said when she stabbed my finger." He held up a bandaged finger as proof.

"She should've told you that would hurt some. But this is just like having your picture taken, but with a different kind of camera—an X-ray machine. Does it hurt to have your picture taken?"

"No," he answered thoughtfully, pushing his small fingers into hers as they walked through the doorway. "Will you stay with me?"

"I have to stand outside the door, but I won't leave," Jenny promised, watching the small figure walk hesitantly into the room.

A few minutes later he emerged, beaming from ear to ear, with a plastic spider clutched in his hand. "It didn't hurt a bit. You didn't lie."

"I told you so." Jenny felt nearly as pleased as Jamie that everything had turned out so well.

"When can I see the picture? Is it a Polaroid?" he asked hopefully.

"It's not quite, but it'll be ready pretty soon. Maybe your doctor will show it to you. Ask him, okay?" Jenny always encouraged the patients to ask their doctors questions, because she felt that it was important for them to know what was happening to them.

After settling Jamie in his room, Jenny went to help Skip get Mrs. Lundy in her wheelchair for a ride to the gift shop.

"How 'bout a cup of cocoa in the cafeteria later on?" Skip asked Jenny.

"Okay." Then he slipped her a copy of *The Lord God Made Them All*, by James Herriott, the English country vet.

"Toby Macey left it for me. I had to remind him I plan on being a people doctor, not an animal one."

Jenny thought immediately of Brian.

* * *

"Hey, where'd you get this?" Brian thumbed delightedly through the book.

"A patient left it," Jenny explained. "Have you read it?"

"No, but I've read all the others. I wanted to get this one, too. Thanks." Brian looked better. His chestnut hair gleamed and curled around his earlobes. It was slightly damp as though he had just washed it.

"You're welcome." Jenny glanced down at Brian's cast where she noticed Skip had scrawled his signature. It sort of looked like the Secret Admirer's handwriting. Could it really be Skip? Then, as she settled into the plastic chair near Brian's bed, she remembered how Roger Bouchet had solicitously walked her to class. She had had the distinct feeling that his interest had been more than casual. It was puzzling all right.

Did Shelly have a clue? Jenny felt that she couldn't discuss it with her at this point. Not after Shelly had practically begged her brother to take her to the prom! Being on nonspeaking terms with your best friend is no fun, Jenny decided. She and Shelly had ridden to the hospital together in stony silence. Shelly had even turned the radio to disco music so loud they couldn't have even screamed above it. Jenny frowned at the memory.

"A penny for your thoughts?" Brian asked, smiling at her. "You looked really weird for a while there. What were you thinking about?"

"Oh, I was just thinking about school," Jenny lied.

They talked about the courses they were taking. Jenny mentioned the upcoming prom, which seemed to make Brian wistful. Maybe she shouldn't have brought it up, she thought later, because when you're lying in a hospital bed, you don't want to hear about people dancing around and having a great time when you can't even walk.

"I'm not going," she told him, thinking that might make him feel better.

"A pretty girl like you?" he teased, but she was flattered that he thought so.

Steve rarely complimented her on her looks. Maybe he was too accustomed to her. Shelly said when you're going with a guy, he usually stops telling you how great you look after a while.

The ride home with Shelly was a little less strained. Shelly squirmed in her seat, finally blurting her news that Jay was coming over when she got home.

"Honest, Jen, I can't stand this. Can't we be friends? I promise not to ruin your life any further."

"Shelly, don't make promises you can't keep," Jenny rebuked. She was still annoyed.

"Oh, come on. You know me—I was just trying to help. Sometimes my help isn't so great, but, well . . . I tried, didn't I? You can't blame me completely."

"Just don't do it again, or I swear I'll disown

you." Jenny wagged a finger at her threateningly, and they both broke into laughter.

"Hey, I saw you in the cafeteria with Skip. Could he be your Secret Admirer?"

"Maybe." It was true, Skip *had* seemed rather more attentive lately, but somehow, it was hard to imagine him in such a role. Still . . . she would have to think about it.

Jenny was surprised to find a bouquet of pink carnations waiting for her on the long-legged entry hall table. Her first thought was that Steve must have sent them to make up for not asking her to the prom.

"Hey, Mom? Dad? Who're these from?" Jenny plucked a tiny card from the bouquet, which was sprigged with stephanotis, too. The scent filled the entire hallway.

Brooke skipped in from the living room. "They're from your Secret Admirer, Jenny. Who is he?"

In disbelief, Jenny consulted the tiny card decorated with gold curlicues. *To Jenny, With Love, Your Secret Admirer.*

"I wish I knew," Jenny whispered, examining the bouquet in case it offered some clue to its origin. "Who delivered it?"

"The florist. Isn't it exciting?"

"Steve swears he didn't send the first note."

"Steve's not romantic enough, anyway," Brooke remarked knowingly.

"What do you know about romance?" Jenny whirled around, suddenly irritable.

"Is he taking you to the prom?" Brooke wanted to know.

"No, but what has that got to do with anything?"

"Now, girls, don't argue. Come and help with dinner."

Mrs. Carlson herded them into the kitchen to take out their aggressions chopping vegetables for the Chinese dish she had planned.

Dr. Carlson was setting the table. "So, you've got an admirer, do you? Any ideas?" He was wearing an old Oakland A's baseball cap that his wife had tried to throw out for years.

"No, Dad. Still a big mystery."

"I know you have admirers at the hospital. Jackie was telling me just yesterday how much she enjoys having you working with her, and that young man, Skip, is by your side every time I turn around."

"Sure, Dad." Jenny sighed, wishing everyone would change the subject—although he was right about Skip. It hadn't been just her imagination, after all.

"It's kinda fun to figure out, isn't it? Like a puzzle or something?" Thad asked her.

Thad was the puzzle hound of the family and, as usual, he was craned over a complicated one, entitled *Reptiles*. It usually took him a few days to complete one, with or without help.

Jenny didn't mention Roger Bouchet to her parents. Nearly everyone she knew, including Roger and Skip, thought of her as Steve's girl. She didn't feel like bringing Roger into the

82

discussion about her Secret Admirer. Besides, it was only a hunch.

"Can you help me with this, Jenny?" Thad entreated, interrupting her thoughts. "The puzzle's too hard for me."

Jenny laughed. "Uncle Bud always sends you games fit for geniuses."

"He ought to lower his standards," Jenny's father added. "Poor Thad's going to be a frustrated genius if we don't watch out."

Jenny had just sat down across from her brother when the phone rang. She stared at the picture. Lizards crawling, one by one, into a jigsaw puzzle to become part of it. What a weird painting!

"Jenny, it's for you." Brooke rolled her eyes expressively. "It's a *boy*. *Steve*."

"Hi. It's me, Steve. Listen." He sounded awfully nervous. "Do you want to go to the prom with me?"

Jenny gasped in disbelief. "The . . . with *you*? Well, sure, but I thought you didn't want to . . . and just because . . ." She wasn't making any sense at all.

"Yeah, well. I changed my mind, okay? I didn't think about it before, but . . . well. So you'll go?"

"Yes, I'd like that." She kept her voice cool, but inside she was screaming I'd love it, love it, love it! If only he knew how much she'd hoped he'd ask.

He cleared his throat. "When you know what color dress you're wearing, let me know."

"Oh, sure. I will." The blue dress floated to the surface of her thoughts, silky and soft, a tangible part of her original dream. "Blue," she whispered to herself.

"What?"

"Oh, nothing."

He didn't need to know she already had a dress picked out. She'd gotten what she wanted even if he'd asked her out of guilt. Still, he was taking her.

She was going to the prom.

6

Is my brother a peach, or isn't he?" Shelly blurted when Jenny told her about her prom invitation.

"He is," confirmed Jenny, beaming. "Will you go shopping with me?"

"Will I? Maybe we can get that red cupcake dress for you."

"Not hardly." Jenny cracked up. "I know which one I want."

It was then that Jenny happened to glance at the centerpiece on the Flemings' dining table. A bouquet of pink carnations just like the ones from her Secret Admirer!

"Where'd the flowers come from?" Jenny ventured.

"Like 'em? One of Mom's clients is a florist. We get a good deal on flowers," Shelly explained.

"Are you sure?"

"What do you mean, am I sure?"

"It's just that those are the same kind of flowers that my Secret Admirer sent me."

"Maybe it's my brother, after all."

"Maybe, but I don't think so." Jenny would like Steve to be the Secret Admirer, but his reaction to it pretty much convinced her he wasn't the one. A sudden thought occurred to her. This was just the kind of prank Shelly loved—matchmaking, playing Cupid. And she was such a good actress, too. "Shelly, you wouldn't be my Secret Admirer, by any chance?"

"Geez, Jen! I love you, but not that much. I swear!"

"It just seems like your style, to try and get me and Steve . . ."

"Hey, why would I bother? My brother's taking you to the prom, isn't he? I don't need to interfere anymore."

"Ha-ha." The Secret Admirer had appeared *before* Steve invited Jenny to the dance, so it still could have been Shelly, Jenny thought to herself. She would have to investigate further. She was sure that eventually he—she?—would give himself (herself?) away.

When Shelly and Jenny got to the department store, Jenny made a beeline for the rack of dresses where she'd admired the blue gown just the other day.

"One thing about you, Jen, you sure know what you want," Shelly commented as Jenny purposefully hiked the dress off the rack. "Nothing wishy-washy about you."

"Listen. I had a sneak preview coming in here with you," she explained, taking two sizes into the dressing room. "Otherwise, I'd try on a whole bunch of them."

There were four other girls from school trying on dresses. Carol McCall, a cheerleader, had on a frothy coral gown with a sharply nipped-in waistline. Letisha Wiseman pranced around the dressing rooms in the red dress that had looked so awful on Shelly, but it seemed to fit Letty's personality. Barbie Springer, a petite, sleek-haired pompon girl, peeled formals on and off in a wild frenzy, searching for the perfect look. She was still looking when Jenny had hers bagged and ready to go.

Angie Morgan peered intently at the racks of gowns, unable to decide what would look right on her slightly plump figure. Jenny took a few moments to help her find something flattering.

Finally, she hit upon a long-sleeved gown in a rich green, cut to a deep V at the throat. "This would be pretty on you, Angie," Jenny suggested. "The neckline will show off your tan, too."

Angie tried it on, and it was just right, smoothing over her hips so that they appeared deceptively slimmer.

"I love it. It's me, isn't it, Jennifer? Oh, thank you so much," she said.

Jenny smiled, pleased that she could help.

There was nothing worse than needing a dress, but not finding exactly what you wanted.

With the beautiful blue gown and a pair of delicate gold high heels, Jenny felt weightless, just like the astronauts must've felt in space. She kept shooting glances at Shelly, unable to stop wondering if the Secret Admirer was just another one of Shelly's crazy ideas.

"Let's go out to lunch to celebrate," Jenny suggested at the spur of the moment. "Everything's turning out so well . . . we're all getting exactly what we want."

Angie laughed. "So we ought to go stick on a few more pounds that we don't want, is that it?"

"Let's insist on a diet lunch."

"I'll just order carrot sticks," Shelly said.

The group walked around the corner to an old-fashioned drugstore where you could always count on a good grilled cheese sandwich and fries, although the two plumper girls insisted on cottage cheese and fruit. Jenny didn't need to watch her weight, yet she felt self-conscious gorging herself in front of the others, so she settled with just the grilled cheese.

"I think Darryl will just love you in that dress," Jenny remarked.

Angie blushed noticeably. "Didn't you hear? I'm not going out with Darryl anymore. This week it's Barry."

Shelly giggled. "When did this change occur?"

"About a month ago, Darryl and I just went our separate ways. And Barry and I became partners on the debate team. You can fill in the rest." Angie smiled radiantly.

"Love at first argument, huh?" Shelly teased.

"I think we need a school newsletter to keep up with the changes in couples on campus," Jenny said. "The newspaper has old class news by the time it's issued." She was thinking of how many changes had taken place in her life since school started in the fall—her job at the hospital, Steve, her schoolwork . . .

When Jenny got home, she checked the flowers again. Sure enough, the carnations were the same shade of pink, with the delicate sprigs of baby's breath framing them— just like the bouquet at Shelly's house.

There was a Cub Scout meeting at Jenny's house. Five noisy boys charged around brandishing paintbrushes, while Maxine blew her whistle, trying to gain their attention.

The other den mother, Toni Ravelli, sat on the patio with three quieter boys, helping them decoupage prints.

"Come see what the boys have done," Maxine called to Jenny, above the din.

"I can already see what they've done," Jenny responded wryly, surveying the sea of wood stain, brushes, sawed pieces of wood and newspaper that were strewn across the patio. What a mess!

Obediently, she strode out to take a look at their handiwork, clutching her purchases possessively against her chest.

"Oh, that looks beautiful, Mark." She complimented a redheaded boy. "Is that going to be a gift for someone?"

"My sister at college," he said, proudly displaying a print of a little girl offering a saucer of milk to a kitten.

"She'll love it," Jenny told him.

Watching her mother round up the rambunctious members of the troop, including her own brother, Jenny thought what a lot of patience her mom must have to put up with this gang. There were a few streaks of white glue stuck in her hair, and her hands—and apron—were mottled with walnut stain.

Jenny hid in her room, grateful for the opportunity to simply stare at her beautiful dress. It was even prettier than she'd expected. The fabric caught the light and sent it dancing across its surface, like moonlight skimming the sea. The softly gathered skirt emphasized her narrow waist. And when she slipped on the gold sandals, she felt like Cinderella must have when she put on the glass slippers—completely transformed.

"You look lovely, Jenny."

Jenny turned around. Her mom stood in the doorway, a sort of breathless look on her face.

"Like it?"

"It's just you." Her mother smiled, and

Jenny felt that everything had to be perfect now.

By Friday, Jenny could hardly contain her excitement. The next night was the dance. At the hospital, she breezed up and down the halls with her cart, so cheerful that the patients eyed her curiously.

"What's the occasion?" Skip teased. "Big date tonight? Oh, I know—Midnight Lace."

Jenny smiled. Did she detect jealousy in his tone?

"Brian's got a visitor. Wow, what a doll! Her name's Elaine," he added.

"Oh, really?" What had she expected? The track star without girlfriend? She was not sure she liked the idea of Brian seeing such a beautiful girl and she knew she didn't care for Skip's open admiration of the visitor. What was the matter with her anyhow? Was she turning into one of those dreadful boy-crazy girls she had always scorned?

Mrs. Durant zeroed right in on Jenny's mood. "Why, Jennifer, darling." She always called everyone "darling," "Are you in love, my dear?"

Jenny blushed three shades of red. "Oh, uh, well, sort of, Mrs. Durant. I'm going to the prom tomorrow night, and I've got this fantastic dress to wear. I guess I'm just excited."

"So you should be. You know, I remember a time when I was a young, beautiful girl like yourself . . ." And off she went into one of her colorful stories of her flapper days, tying

Jenny up for the next fifteen or twenty minutes.

Not that she minded. Mrs. Durant was one of the most interesting people in the whole hospital. Jenny was still giggling when she walked into Brian's room.

"What's up? You're sure in a good mood tonight," Brian remarked. He sat up straighter, running his fingers through his hair.

"Have you ever met Mrs. Durant?" she asked. He nodded. "She's a little old lady down the hall from you with a broken hip, and we were talking about the prom, and then she started telling me about her flapper days. . . ."

"Are you going to the prom?" Brian asked quietly. Their eyes met.

"Yes, with my boyfriend," Jenny explained.

"My girlfriend and I were going to go to our winter prom, but we won't now. My friend, Jay Sheldon, is going."

"With my friend, Shelly." Jenny swallowed hard, not wanting to make Brian feel bad. Everybody going but him—how awful! Anxious to change the subject, she said, "You should meet Mrs. Durant, if you get the chance. I bet she was a riot when she was our age."

Brian laughed. "Sounds as though she still is." He rolled the hem of his sheet between his thumb and forefinger. Jenny noticed his square-cut nails, and the long, tanned fingers which she could easily visualize gently tending a hurt animal.

"Hey, I met your father today," he said.

"Oh, really?"

"He was with my doctor, Dr. Menkin. A really nice guy. You're lucky to have him."

"I think so."

"He said this job is really making you blossom." Brian's eyes narrowed as he scrutinized her. "What do you think?"

Jenny shrugged, not knowing quite how to answer. "Oh, I don't know. I like what I do and I'm learning a lot." She paused. "When do you leave?" she asked.

"Sunday. It'll be nice to get out of here." He fingered the plastic bracelet on his arm as he glanced around the room. "Will you come see me Sunday morning?"

Suddenly, Jenny realized how important her visits were to him. Figuring he had lots of friends, including a girlfriend, she had never wanted to come by too often. It might seem funny.

Brian must've guessed what she was thinking, for he said, "You know, when you first go into hospital, all these people come to see you—friends and family—always family. You get more attention than you ever got in your whole life and you don't feel up to it. Then, by the time you feel better, the friends drop off. They don't come by as much, or hardly at all. They figure you'll be home soon, so why bother?

"One of the guys here, Brad Nettleton, told me after you get home, it's worse. Nobody comes to see you. You just sit around watching reruns on TV, and talk to your folks. Life just goes on around you, and you're stuck in one place watching it happen." He gave her a sheepish smile, which Jenny found strangely attractive. "Sorry, I didn't mean to bore you."

"You're not boring me. You're telling me like it is. There's nothing boring about that." She wanted to ask *What about your girlfriend?* but instead, she said, "You just had a visitor, didn't you?"

"Oh, yeah. My girlfriend." He grinned at her, his eyes full of mischief. "She crochets and talks to me at the same time."

Involuntarily, Jenny's gaze followed the outline of his lips, the sharp curve of cheekbones, the stunning blue eyes framed by dark lashes.

"I wish I could be at that dance." Brian smiled at her. "You know, I'm not a bad dancer, myself."

"Oh, yeah?"

"Yeah." Jenny noticed the change in his expression as he looked down at his leg.

"Listen, Brian, you'll dance circles around everybody once you get out of this place."

"You better believe it," he said with conviction.

Jenny placed her hand over his, a gesture that ordinarily might have seemed too forward, but at that moment, it seemed right.

He opened his fingers and let hers slide down between them into a kind of handshake. The warmth and feel of his skin, roughly sensual, brought quick tears to her eyes.

"I'd better go, Brian," she said, drawing her hand away. "I've got work to do."

"See you Sunday." He winked.

"Sunday," she said.

She skipped into the hall. An image of herself in Brian's arms, gliding across the dance floor, those piercing blue eyes gazing down into hers, formed in her mind.

She shook the picture away. After Sunday, she probably wouldn't see Brian again. He didn't even go to the same school! Maybe once in a while, they'd run into each other at football games. That was about it. Besides, why should she even think about that? Brian had a girlfriend and she was going to the prom with Steve.

Jenny sat in front of her vanity mirror, experimenting with combs which she had few opportunities to wear. She let her hair fluff close to one cheek, and drew a tuft of it back on the other side, securing it with a gold and blue painted comb.

"There! How does that look?"

Jenny turned on the needlepoint seat to get Brooke's reaction.

"Dynamite." Brooke sighed, draping herself across Jenny's bed. "I can't wait until I get to go to a prom," she added wistfully.

"Oh, you'll go to plenty. More than me, I'm sure."

"You think so?" Brooke slid off the bed to examine her cherubic face in the mirror.

"Sure I do. Now watch out—don't bump my elbow," Jenny warned as she applied mascara.

"I take that all back—what I said about Steve," Brooke said solemnly. "I think he really is romantic. He just doesn't want anyone to know it. That's why he sends you all that Secret Admirer stuff."

"Maybe," she replied absently, not letting her sister know how valuable her opinion was.

"You look like a princess," Brooke announced, watching Jenny slip an embroidered shawl over her shoulders.

"Thank you, Brooke." She leaned over to kiss Brooke on the top of the head.

"Just be sure to get home in time, so you don't turn into a pumpkin," Brooke shrieked with glee.

Jenny flung a makeup sponge at her. "Oh, you. Maybe Steve's Toyota will turn into one, but I won't."

Feeling confident, Jenny sailed into the living room. Her dad had the camera all set up, ready to take pictures.

"Man, I've never seen you look so good," exclaimed Thad.

Dr. Carlson beamed. "You look wonderful, Jen, really sensational." He snapped away with his camera before she could pose. Those were the pictures her dad liked best anyway—the candid ones. "That Brian Halsey I met yesterday thought a lot of you, you know."

Brian . . . thought a lot of me? The words danced in her mind, riding on the wave of her excitement for the evening ahead.

The doorbell rang. Brooke scrambled to answer it. Jenny was so wound up she was close to crying.

Steve entered, carrying a small white florist's box in which a large blue orchid rested. He cleared his throat nervously. "You look nice, Jenny," he said.

"So do you, Steve." Funny how, dressed up like this, they were acting like mechanical dolls with each other, she thought. Steve was wearing a powder-blue shirt and tux, a carnation threaded through his buttonhole. He looked really handsome, his blond hair slicked down, fresh wet comb tracks running through it.

Nervously, he tried to pin Jenny's corsage to the dress, nearly jabbing her with the pin.

"It's fine, Steve, really," she said as it hung lopsided over her chest. When he wasn't looking, she quickly readjusted it so that it looked right.

"Have a good time!" her parents chimed in the doorway.

Carefully, Jenny tucked the folds of satiny blue skirt into the car.

"You look really nice," Steve kept repeating, as if he couldn't believe it.

He doesn't want to be doing this, Jenny thought fearfully. He was acting overly polite, and stiff—as if the rented clothes were choking the life out of him. What was wrong? Was it because Shelly practically forced him to ask me? she thought. If he hadn't asked me, I would've thought he was a nerd—is that it? The car nosed into a parking slot at the restaurant.

Melvyn's Steakhouse was a pretty unglamorous name for a nice restaurant. Steve had picked it out because other friends who were going to the prom suggested it. They both ordered thick steaks, which came with a baked potato and salad. Jenny was really hungry, but Steve picked at his dinner.

"Steve? What's wrong? You usually eat enough for both of us," she said.

He shrugged, then waved to a friend at another table.

"I dunno, Jenny. This just isn't my style, I guess." He glanced at the wine-colored walls where candlelight flickered romantically. "You want dessert?"

Mindful of how much this was costing Steve, Jenny declined—even though the dessert tray looked delicious. He seemed anxious to leave.

As they wove through the tables, Jenny saw some friends, about six people, all eating together, laughing and telling jokes. She longed to be part of their group. Why couldn't she and Steve have as much fun?

On the way to the dance, they had little to say to one another. Jenny was panicky by the time they stepped over the threshold of the school gym. Maybe, in this different environ-

ment, with the band and friends and atmosphere, Steve would loosen up.

"Have you heard this band before?" she
asked him. "They're the Sneakers."

"Never heard of 'em. I guess they only play
for things like *this*." He put a disdainful em-
phasis on "this."

"Hey, look at the decorations! Aren't they
pretty?"

A lacy canopy draped the stage, and the
walls were covered with dark maroon materi-
al with lace panels on top. Top hats and canes
were hung jauntily on that background, giving the room an old-fashioned flavor. Adding
authenticity were the band members decked
out in top hats and tails.

"Don't you love the outfits?" Shelly greeted
them. She and Jay had their arms wrapped
around each other's waists.

I wish Steve and I were that close, Jenny
thought enviously. "Aren't they super? I think
the guys should've rented top hats for this
dance."

Steve scowled. "Isn't a tux bad enough?" he
grumbled.

Just then, the lights dimmed and the band
took off with a rollicking number. The music
began to unravel some of the little knots
inside Jenny, but she still felt uptight, wondering how Steve would like the music, and if
he were having a good time or not. Why did
she fear the very worst?

She danced mechanically, trying not to appear as if she were searching Steve's face for

his reaction. She thought of Brian with that teasing look in his eyes. How he longed to be able to dance like this!

Steve took her hand and they swung into the next number, without breaking stride. At last, he looked as though he were beginning to get into it. Jenny began to relax a little more, even though her date didn't exactly look overjoyed.

Roger Bouchet waved cheerfully at her. He was dancing with Marjorie DeVries, the foreign-exchange student from France. Eddie Isaacson and Terri Billings were doing their punk rock routine—complete with splits and floor spins. Terri was wearing a crazy, orange chiffon formal, which, when she dropped on the floor for the splits, pleated into a rainbow of different colors. They were such a show-stopper that everyone cleared the dance floor to watch them.

When that dance ended, Angie Morgan threaded her way towards Jenny and Steve.

"Angie, you look great," Jenny exclaimed.

Angie had her hair up in an exotic twist with little tendrils escaping artfully at the sides. And her dress looked even better under the muted lights.

"Thanks," Angie said. "And thanks for helping me pick it out. I love yours."

"What is this?" countered Steve. "The mutual admiration society here? All you girls wanna do is tell each other how great you look. What about us guys?"

"You all look great too," Angie said. "It's

nice to see you in something other than T-shirts and jeans."

"Just like my mother," Steve groaned good-naturedly.

Jenny was relieved to see he was shedding his grumpy mood.

After Angie sailed back to her date, a square-faced, beefy-looking guy named Teddy Rawlins, Steve prodded Jenny. "Hey, is that what you've been doing—helping everybody choose their prom dresses, huh?"

"No, just Angie. She was in the store when I went to get my dress, and she was having trouble choosing."

They were slow dancing, and Steve's lips moved against Jenny's hair, sending a tingle down her spine.

"Yeah, I bet. But she looks great tonight. Did she lose weight, too?"

"Maybe." Jenny didn't want to say too much about Angie to Steve. It didn't seem fair to discuss her weight problems with him.

There were two switching-partners dances, and Roger asked Jenny.

"You look really pretty, Jenny," he whispered admiringly. "And your corsage looks familiar."

"What?" She looked down at the orchid pinned to her dress.

He laughed. "We make those up. My father's a florist. Never heard of Bouchet's Florist Shop?"

"Really?" Jenny gasped. Of course she'd

heard of it, but had never put Roger's name with the shop. He watched her, amusement playing across his features. So Roger was the Secret Admirer! It all made sense now.

She went back to Steve, hoping the secret didn't show in her smile. She wondered if Roger knew she knew. Even though she didn't like Roger as a boyfriend, it was exciting to know that he liked her enough to do such a thing. Knowing that made her evening even more magical.

Jenny wanted to dance only with Steve all night. She'd dreamed of coming with him for so long, and here she was, twirling about in his arms, his breath against her cheek, the scents of her perfume and his cologne mingling together as one. Jenny loved every minute of it, and as the night wore on, they danced slower, stopping occasionally to kiss or simply hug each other close.

"I didn't think I'd have a good time tonight," Steve confessed.

"Yeah, I know. But look, we were one of the last couples to leave."

They were snuggled together in the car, overlooking the beach and the black expanse of ocean beyond. The foghorn bleated its mournful warning into the night, and every other second the lighthouse beacon cast a wand of light across Steve and Jenny's faces. Steve pulled off his bow tie, revealing a wedge of tanned throat, and tipped Jenny's face to meet his.

"I feel that I've been under a spell," Steve murmured as he helped Jenny out of the car at her house. "Thanks for the good time."

His mouth covered hers before she could answer. The night sounds faded behind them as they stood holding each other in the darkness.

7

Jenny hurried—vacuuming, dusting—trying to straighten up the house for her mother's charity luncheon that afternoon. She wanted to see Brian before he checked out of the hospital, so she was working at top speed when the telephone rang.

"Hi. This is Roger Bouchet. Remember me?" He sounded uncomfortable.

"Hi, Roger. I haven't forgotten you. Did you have a good time at the dance?" Jenny suppressed a giggle at the thought of forgetting Roger.

"Sure did. Um, I was wondering . . . would you like to go to a movie with me next Friday night?"

She was glad Roger couldn't see her. She'd never had to turn anyone down before, and she wasn't exactly sure what to say. "Thanks for asking me, Roger. But I'm going with someone. You know, Steve Fleming?"

"Oh, yeah, right. Well, I figured I'd try . . . you didn't say for sure, you know." He fumbled to close the conversation, then finally hung up.

Jenny leaned back against the wall, feeling strange. Did Roger think she wasn't going with Steve anymore? What would give him that idea? she wondered.

The phone jangled, making her jump.

"Who were you talking to?" Shelly demanded. She always acted as though Jenny'd committed a crime if she tied up the line too long.

"Roger Bouchet. He asked me out."

"No kidding? Didn't he see you last night with Steve? What nerve that guy has!"

"He said he was just checking." Now Jenny wished she'd never mentioned it. "Did you have a good time last night?"

"Did we ever! Jay is the greatest . . ." Shelly wanted to talk forever, analyze every detail of the night before. But if she were to get to the hospital in time, Jenny considered, she had to finish her work.

"Listen, Shelly, I've gotta go. My mom's having a luncheon here today and I've got to clean for her."

"Maybe I'll see you later, huh?" Shelly sounded disappointed.

"Sure."

Jenny hung up, turned on the dishwasher, put fresh flowers in the center of the dining table, stuffed the vacuum cleaner in the hall closet, grabbed her sweater and hurried out to her bike.

Jenny charged down the hall of the orthopedic floor, coming to a skidding halt outside Brian's room. Catching her breath, she saw him poised on the edge of the bed facing the window, talking on the phone.

She took one step into the room, then stopped in her tracks.

". . . yeah, Mom, now don't forget . . . okay? I'm fine, fine . . . just get me outta here."

Jenny memorized his back, taut and muscular in his white T-shirt. She liked the way he threw back his head when he laughed, which he did often. She liked how he sat, hunched forward, absorbed in his conversation, his elbow casually propped on his thigh.

Jenny was so absorbed watching Brian that she jumped at the gentle tap on her shoulder.

"Mr. Rice!"

"I'm glad I caught you, Jenny. Going-home day for me, did you know?" He winked at her, blue eyes nearly lost in the crinkles.

"You better be careful, Mr. Rice. No more fooling around." She wagged a finger at him, giggling.

"I told you . . . as soon as this cast comes off, I'm going hang gliding! You're never too young to try a new sport, you know." He wagged a crutch at her. "See you, Jenny."

"'Bye, Mr. Rice. And be careful!" Mr. Rice's

booming laughter echoed through the hall-way. Jenny strolled into Brian's room.

"Hey, Jenny!" His face brightened when she walked through the door. "I wasn't sure you were gonna make it."

"Hi, Brian," she greeted him. "Going-home day, huh?"

"Yeah, I can't wait . . . except I wanted to see you first."

A slow warmth spread through Jenny's limbs. How special he is . . . *and he wanted to see me first—before leaving!*

She watched him hoist himself onto his crutches. "See? I'm getting the hang of these things. Pretty soon, I'll be running races."

She laughed. "I can just see you swinging down the halls at school."

"I hope. Maybe I can't beat 'em at track, but they haven't got a load of me on crutches yet." His eyes held hers for a moment. "Did you have fun last night?"

"Oh, the dance. Yeah, it was fun." Jenny was surprised to find that she had almost forgotten about it. She didn't even feel like talking about it that much. "Good music," she forced herself to say. "Ever heard of the Sneakers?"

"Sure. My brother knows the drummer."

"Really?"

"Aren't you impressed?" He laughed and hopped around the room on his crutches. "Will I see you after I leave here? I mean, I'm sure you're really busy, but maybe I can give you a call sometime."

Jenny smiled tentatively. "What'll your girl-friend think?" she asked.

"My girlfriend." He looked thoughtful. "She doesn't have to know, and if she does find out, I'll tell her you're a friend."

He pawed through his wallet until he located one of his mother's business cards, and underlined his home phone number. She noticed Skip's signature on the cast again. Could he be the one? "Now, don't call the office, unless you're interested in insurance."

Jenny giggled. A tall, slender woman with the same chestnut curls as Brian stepped into the room. Brian introduced Jenny to his mother as "the girl who made my hospital stay bearable."

They all laughed.

"It was nice meeting you, Mrs. . . ." Panicked, Jenny realized she'd forgotten Brian's last name.

"Halsey," supplied his mother, with a warm smile. "Thanks for taking such good care of him, Jenny. I've heard nothing but good reports about you."

Jenny blushed, protesting. "Oh, I didn't do anything, honest." She got up to leave, not wanting to be in the way. " 'Bye, Brian."

"Take it easy, Jenny. And remember what I said." He held up one hand in a wave, and shot her a lopsided grin.

Jenny hurried down the hall, nearly colliding with the dark-haired girl, Elaine—Brian's girlfriend. Carrying a package under one arm, Elaine glided confidently into Brian's room.

Jenny's heart sank. For an instant, she wanted Brian's arms around her, she wanted to bury her face in his broad shoulder. What was the matter with her anyway? Hadn't she just starred in her ultimate dream by going to the prom with Steve? I must have a split personality, she decided, pedaling furiously away from Shiloh.

The Carlsons' home was full of people when Jenny got home. Unfortunately, there was no graceful way of sneaking into the house without weaving through a crowd, and everyone had to stop her and say hello and ask how school was.

Jenny listened politely to the descriptions of what their teenagers were doing, wondering how her mom could stand all this idle talk for an entire afternoon.

No sooner had she made the escape to her bedroom when Mrs. Carlson tracked her down. "Jenny—can you help me, please? I need someone to dish up the crepes."

"Sure, Mom." Reluctantly, Jenny went out to the kitchen to begin dishing up the seemingly endless plates of food. Nearly every woman in the room was yakking about being on a diet, but they were all prepared to gobble up the delicious turkey crepes her mom had made.

She wondered what Brian was doing right

now. It was funny how, when he had been in the hospital, she'd never thought about his activities, probably because he was so limited there. She wondered where he lived, and what his house looked like—but most of all, she wondered how he felt about her.

"Jenny! Steve is here," her mother announced coolly. "You didn't ask him over, did you?"

"No, Mom. Don't worry—I wouldn't do that." The disapproval on Mrs. Carlson's face relaxed. "I'll go outside and talk to him."

Steve was sitting on the front step. His hair was damp and he was wearing his wetsuit.

"Hi. What are you doing here?" Jenny asked, wiping her hands down the front of her faded apron.

When he turned to face her, his eyes blazed into her own. "Shelly told me about Roger Bouchet," he said sarcastically. "Why didn't you tell me you liked him?"

"I never . . ." Jenny gasped in horrified surprise. "I like Roger for a *friend*, Steve. I never said I liked him any other way. He asked me out, that was all. What did your sister tell you, anyway?"

"She said he asked you out. He knows you're going with me, right? Why did he do that, unless he figured you'd go?"

"He didn't know for sure whether we were still together." Jenny found herself defending Roger. "But I told him we were, so there's nothing to worry about. He won't ask me again."

110

"Yeah, sure." Steve's scowl deepened noticeably. "He's gotta be your loony Secret Admirer."

"I guess so." Jenny shrugged helplessly. "It sounds as though you don't trust me. I don't think that's fair."

"Ha. Look who's talking about fair," he snapped. Rising, he left a wet imprint on the porch step. Leaning over, he swept a little hill of sand from the cement. "I'm not dense, you know."

"I know." She reached out for his hand, but he took a step backward. "Look, I can't control other people's feelings. Don't get mad at me just because Roger likes me."

"Oh, yeah? Don't try and con me, Jenny. I know you liked getting all that attention. Who wouldn't?" In spite of his fierceness, Steve's expression crumpled into hurt, miserable lines.

"Steve, I like you the way you are. I never wanted you to change. . . ." Jenny swallowed hard, remembering all the times she'd wished Steve would do this, or say that. But she couldn't tell him that. She had to smooth things over, let him know everything was okay.

Finally, she suggested going for a walk.

He looked at her as though she were crazy. "In my wetsuit?"

"We'll take the trail through the woods. No one will see you."

Barely convinced, he slipped on his thongs and followed her along the footpath that

111

wound down into a canyon behind Jenny's house.

It was remote, private, and their voices absorbed into the rich quiet of the woods. Bluejays cawed and hopped among the high pine branches; unseen creatures scuttled around in the underbrush.

"I liked the attention, Steve, but that doesn't mean anything has to change between you and me," Jenny said. Her voice had taken on a pleading tone which she fought to control. "There won't be any more Secret Admirers, I'm sure. One in a lifetime's enough for anyone, isn't it?"

Steve's face softened. "Yeah, I guess you're right. I'm just jealous, though. I want you all to myself."

Somewhere, somehow, Jenny felt a hairline crack in their relationship—or maybe it had been there all the time. She didn't know. But it was just wide enough to admit thoughts of somebody else—namely Brian—traitorous, scary thoughts which Jenny was afraid Steve might sense.

"I had fun at the dance last night," she said, shaking off her fearfulness enough to coax a smile out of him.

"Yeah, me too. I was surprised. I mean"—instantly he tried to amend what he'd said, looking apologetic—"since my sister was the one who started it."

"So I really was dragging you there by the hair, huh?" Jenny laughed, but her insides felt brittle and turned upside down. "The truth comes out."

He never did want to take her to the dance—he'd gone only because of Shelly—just as Jenny had suspected all along.

Suddenly, her carefully constructed fantasy came apart at the seams. Steve had felt forced into the role of her date, had gone along with the whole thing just to please her. She should've known that you can't force a situation on anyone, especially somebody like Steve who had strong ideas of his own.

"Hey, Jen, don't look like that. I had a good time, didn't I?" He reached for her hand and squeezed it.

She offered a weak smile. He grinned as if they had come to some kind of understanding, but Jenny got the feeling that they were missing each other by a mile.

"I wondered if you were free this weekend." Skip Trybom sounded so serious over the phone, not like his usual, nutty self.

"What for?" Jenny asked, then realized her tactlessness too late.

"Maybe we could, uh, see a movie."

"I'm going with someone, Skip, I'm sorry. So I guess I'll have plans." Tears welled up behind her eyes. After fighting with Steve, Skip's offer sounded good, but it was out of the question.

"Why didn't you say so? I mean, I thought . . ." He regained his composure, acting nonchalant. "I just thought maybe you were free."

"Thanks for asking, Skip," Jenny said softly. How she hated to hurt his feelings! She just hoped this wouldn't change their friendship. Although by this time she had pretty much decided that Roger was the Secret Admirer, now she began to wonder again about Skip. He had never asked her for a date before.

8

I heard you come in late last night," Evan reported when Jenny went out to talk to him after Steve left. He was oiling the lawnmower, getting ready to do his and her parents' lawn.

Jenny stared at her scuffed running shoes as if they held sudden interest. "It was fun," she said.

"But arguing with Steve this afternoon wasn't, was it?" he prodded.

She frowned under his scrutiny. "Since when did you get so smart?"

"Since I've been over here spying on you for the past few months."

"Oh, yeah? Is that what you've been doing?"

"Yeah. As a matter of fact, you're a pretty interesting subject."

"Is that so?" Jenny grew thoughtful. An idea popped into her mind that she hadn't thought of before. Maybe Evan was her Secret Admirer. "Evan . . ."

"Hmmm?" He was engrossed in his motor.

"You wouldn't happen to know who my Secret Admirer is, would you?"

He straightened to his full height and shook his head. "Nope. Personally, I don't make my admiration of you a secret. I think you're the greatest, and I'm not afraid to tell you to your face."

"Thanks." Jenny leaned forward and gave him a light peck on the cheek.

He blushed. "I should give you compliments more often."

"You deserve an award for being the most honest person I know," Jenny told him.

"Oh, yeah?" He cocked his head to one side. "So you really have a Secret Admirer?"

"Yes. He sends me flowers and notes . . ."

"How exciting. You're Miss Popularity, huh?"

"Come on, Evan. Be serious."

"It's not Steve, huh?"

"No."

He leaned over the lawnmower, bracing himself to start the engine. "Figures. Steve's not really the romantic type. And why would he do all that, anyway? You're already his girl."

Jenny remembered how romantic Steve had seemed last night, and how deceived she had been. No, that wasn't right—he hadn't deceived her. She had deceived herself into believing he wanted to take her to the dance.

"I think it's Roger," she said.

"Could be Roger. Roger's a definite possibility."

Jenny backed off when the lawnmower roared to life. Evan waved to her as he ran the mower across the front lawn. She stood in the driveway, watching, and thinking that now she didn't care who the Secret Admirer was. If he wasn't Steve, the only other person she would like it to be was Brian: but Brian had a girlfriend, so that eliminated him. I really like him, she thought, surprising and frightening herself at the same time.

What am I thinking? I wanted to go to the prom with Steve, I got what I wanted, and now I know the way I got it wasn't what I wanted. What do I want, anyway? she quizzed herself.

Evan cut the engine. "Maybe the guy at the hospital is the one."

"Brian has a girlfriend," Jenny explained.

"Oh." She followed him into the house for lemonade and mentioned that Skip had asked her out.

"Perhaps it's Skip?" Evan suggested.

Jenny sighed, finishing off her lemonade. "Actually, I don't care who he is now," she said. "I'm sick of thinking about it."

"I don't believe it," Evan said. "I know how it is. Once I'm told not to think about something, that's all I can think about."

"You're so philosophical."

"I have to be." Evan ate eight oatmeal cookies in succession. "By the way, if you want to run off some of your frustrations later, I'm game."

"Thanks. I think I have about four miles' worth," Jenny laughed. "Let me know when you're done."

Jenny invited Evan to come and watch the last volleyball game of the season—the championship game, in which the Royals were pitted against Marcia Bracken's team, the Bulldogs, the fiercest team in school.

Steve came, too. Jenny felt she had to be careful not to talk to Evan too much before the game because Steve might get upset. She was annoyed to constantly have to make room for Steve's unreasonableness in everything she did—even talking to a dear friend whom she'd known since grammar school. What right did he have to expect that from her? She slammed the ball into the left-hand corner.

Her well-placed serve resulted in a volley that gave the Royals another point. Honestly, there might be something to Doris's and Millie's theories about boys. She was beginning to wonder if there was room for friendship in a romance, or—the thought seemed nearly dangerous—if she and Steve really had a romance. She still hadn't recovered from the fact that he felt forced to take her to the dance. And no matter how politely she behaved to his face, it still burned her up.

The ball sailed across the net once more. Sue Billings punched it straight into the air

118

and out of bounds. One more point for the Royals. The crowd went crazy.

Besides, every time Jenny glimpsed Shelly's profile as they were playing, she got mad. How dare Shelly tell Steve she thought Roger was the Secret Admirer! Sometimes Shelly went a little too far . . .

Jenny glanced over at the bleachers and noticed that Steve was gone. Maybe he had gone to get a drink. She wasn't really concerned. In fact, tension oozed out of her pores, making her loose-limbed, freer.

The audience was largely composed of boys —whom she recognized as boyfriends of team members. The ball spiraled towards her. Jenny socked it over the net, a fast hit that the Bulldogs couldn't retrieve. The score hit thirteen to five, in the Royals' favor.

It didn't take much longer for the Royals to score the additional two points that gave them the championship. The team went absolutely crazy.

"Jenny, you were tremendous!" Evan hugged her unabashedly on the court.

"Thanks, I feel great," she replied, grinning. Out of the corner of her eye, she spotted Steve coming towards them. She broke away from Evan and went to him.

"I missed the last part, but I heard you were great," Steve said, looking from Evan to Jenny.

Jenny ignored the look. "It was a super game."

"Want some popcorn?" Steve thrust a box of popcorn at her.

"No, thanks," she declined. "I'm going out with the team for refreshments. I'll see you later."

Steve frowned. Jenny exhaled uneasily as she hurried to join the Royals, anxious to reinfect herself with their high spirits.

Shelly went off with Jay instead of joining the team at Wellington's Ice Cream Parlor after the game. Jenny was relieved—she didn't want to confront her friend yet about her telling Steve about Roger.

"Here's to our powers of concentration!" Millie shouted, knocking her ice cream sundae glass against everyone else's.

"Cheers."

"Did you notice how many boys turned out to watch this game?" Doris added, eyes shining. "Nat was there."

"He only had eyes for you, Doris," Jenny put in.

"What happened to Steve, Jenny?" Millie took her aside to ask.

"He missed the last part. I guess his powers of concentration are not as great as ours," Jenny replied with a twinge of bitterness. "We haven't been getting along that well . . ."

"You looked like you were doing great at the prom." Millie studied her closely.

"We were. Oh, it's a long story, Millie." Jenny sighed. "Too long and tedious to go into when we're celebrating our victory."

Millie smiled. "Yeah, maybe you're right. Maybe we oughta discuss your love life in the locker room."

Jenny laughed. "Let's discuss yours. There's probably more to discuss."

"There isn't. Since Eddie and I broke up, I'm not seeing anyone, so I have no headaches. I don't have to worry if he's going to call, or if we have a date Friday night. Trouble free."

"Sounds nice. Steve is jealous of every guy I'm friends with," lamented Jenny.

"That's no good. That really cramps your style, Jen. You can't let him do that to you."

"I thought we weren't going to discuss my love life?" Jenny said.

"We couldn't resist just mentioning it." Millie giggled.

Marcia Bracken and her Bulldogs entered Wellington's at that moment. Marcia broke away from the others to bestow her grudging best on Millie. "Good team, Millie. You deserve it." The words were forced out between gritted teeth. It was a well-known fact that Marcia was not the greatest sport around.

"Thanks, Marcia. You were terrific." Millie shook Marcia's hand. "I'll buy you an ice cream sundae—any kind."

"Thanks. I'll do the same for you next time we win—which will be the next time we play you." Marcia's belligerent tone was somewhat softened by a grudging smile.

9

What's that supposed to be?" Shelly leaned over Jenny's shoulder to peer at the drawing she was working on. A bowl of fruit on Mr. Waite's desk was the model for the sketch.

"A pear. What do you think? Now would you please mind your own business, Shelly?" Jenny demanded in exasperation. "There's nothing worse than having someone staring over your shoulder."

"You need guidance," Shelly teased. "That pear looks like a pregnant apple."

"Oh, cool it, will you? You know I'm no Picasso, for crying out loud."

Jenny had signed up for Art I, thinking it would be an easy class, but it wasn't easy for her. She didn't have an eye for drawing at all, no matter how much Mr. Waite insisted that anyone could draw.

Yet today, art wasn't the reason she was out

of sorts. All morning, Jenny had avoided confronting Shelly about the Steve and Roger thing, and even though she kept trying to convince herself that it wasn't Shelly's fault, secretly she thought it was. Shelly must know it, too, Jenny figured, because she walks around me as though she were afraid of the worst.

"Look at mine," Shelly instructed. "Now you've got to get that curve right."

"Yes, Mother," quipped Jenny.

Mr. Waite frowned in the direction of the two girls, his eyebrows coming together in one long, disapproving line. Hastily, Jenny bowed her head over her work.

"Girls, let's get back to work. This isn't a social hour," Mr. Waite informed them.

Shelly giggled into her palm. It was okay for her to laugh, Jenny thought, she was really talented in art. She could whip up a likeness of someone or something so quickly, it made Mr. Waite's head spin. He was even talking about finding Shelly a summer job drawing caricatures, which she was really excited about.

"Okay, Jenny—I'm sorry, really sorry," Shelly blurted as they stepped out of the art room. "I know you're mad at me, but please don't be. . . ."

"Why do you keep interfering in my life? What did I ever do to you? Didn't you promise me you wouldn't blab to Steve anymore?" Jenny's anger burbled out in a rush.

Shelly hung her head. "Yeah, something like that."

"Why didn't you keep your promise? Is that so hard to do?" Her voice rose to a squeak. "Steve was really mad at me—he actually thought I liked Roger, and that I was leading him on!"

"I'm sorry."

"You should be. Why didn't you call me yesterday after he came over?" Jenny demanded, her head throbbing wildly. She'd never had all these problems before, and now it seemed that her whole life was one big tangle.

"I was scared you'd yell at me the way you're doing now," Shelly explained meekly.

Jenny sighed and took a long look at her friend. It really wasn't Shelly's fault. Words just had a way of flying from Shelly's lips before she knew what was happening, but that didn't mean she wasn't a good friend. "It's my turn to be sorry," Jenny said.

"Look, Jen, I know I meddle in everybody's business too much. It's just that, I guess you shouldn't tell me anything. That way you're safe."

"Whoever heard of a best friend you can't talk to?"

"Yeah, well, I just thought my brother takes you for granted too much, and he ought to see that other guys are interested. Gets him a little jealous. It keeps him on his toes."

"It gets him jealous, for sure, but it also hurt his feelings." Were Steve's feelings really hurt, or did he just dislike the idea of other guys showing interest in Jenny?

"What's *wrong* with that? I thought you'd be happy to have him crazy about you, and jealous of any guy that looked at you." Shelly studied her with concern. "I'd want Jay to like me that much."

"Yeah, I guess you're right."

"Do you like Roger?"

"Sure, as a friend, Shelly. That's what I told Steve, and it's true. Roger knows I'm Steve's girlfriend."

It was the first time Jenny had said it aloud —even though she always wanted to think of the two of them as a couple, she had been slightly afraid to. Steve was the one who had never made the commitment, never voiced his feelings, but now that he was beginning to let her know how he felt, she wasn't sure. . . .

"So now you've got nothing to worry about. No more Secret Admirer, right?" Shelly grinned broadly.

Jenny bit her lip over a confession. She was beginning to carry more secrets than the Secret Admirer himself.

"Want to come in for a snack?" Jenny asked Steve. They were parked in front of her house.

"Yeah, sure. Just for a minute, then I'm going surfing," he said, motioning to the black wetsuit huddled in the corner of the backseat.

"It looks like a discarded skin."

"It's my water skin."

From the entry hall, Jenny glimpsed a big white box on the dining table, a blue ribbon dangling from a piece of Scotch tape on its side.

"Jenny! Hi, Steve. How are you?" Mrs. Carlson greeted them, cradling a tiny cream-colored Siamese kitten in her arms. Two sapphire eyes blinked inquisitively at Jenny and Steve.

"Isn't she beautiful?" Jenny cooed, reaching for her, forgetting everything. "Where'd you get her?"

"She's really yours, Jen. She came in that box—from your Secret Admirer." Her mother's eyes sparkled mischievously. "I had to open it, the meows were so plaintive. I couldn't leave the poor kitty in there for another minute."

Brian raises Siamese kittens . . . was it really him? But he has a girlfriend. . . . Jenny's head whirled.

"What do you think of all this, Steve?" Mrs. Carlson asked.

Suddenly, Jenny wished she could disappear, fold herself into that big white box with all her doubts and fears and the little kitten and not have to deal with what was going to happen next.

The kitten placed two chocolate paws delicately on Jenny's shirt sleeve and sniffed the air tentatively. She must have sniffed out the danger, because Steve was fuming.

"It's crazy," he said, his face contorted into a stiff, angry mask.

126

Jenny breathed shakily. "Here, Mom. Take the kitty. Excuse us."

She thrust the kitten in her mother's arms and led the way to the backyard, stopping at the swing set.

Steve stuck his thumbs in his beltloops and just stared at her. "Okay, what's going on? Spit it out. I'm dying to hear all about it."

Jenny sat on the creaky wooden swing, her palms slippery against the cold metal links. "Look, Steve, I was honest with you before, and I'm being honest with you now, okay? I'm just as surprised as you about this. First I thought you were the Secret Admirer, and then—"

"We went through this before," he cut in roughly. "And then you figured it was Roger, right? I thought you said you gave Roger the brush-off."

He said that so unkindly. In fact, there were a lot of things Steve said that she didn't like, but she let them go. It was just as unkind, she figured, to dwell on people's faults. "I don't think it's Roger."

Steve's mouth fell open in surprise. "It's *not* Roger? *Who is it*? This is really getting interesting—better than a soap opera."

"Listen, I don't have to tell you if I don't want to. You're really being a nerd."

"Me?"

Jenny faced Steve. Why was he being so unreasonable? "For a while I thought Shelly was doing this as one of her little matchmaking stunts, then I thought it might be Skip Trybom at the hospital or Roger because he works at his dad's florist shop. But now I'm pretty sure it's one of the orthopedic patients."

Steve was sitting on a stone planter with his chin propped in his hands, looking like a sulking *Thinker*. Suddenly, he rose, blood filling his face. "And you acted as though you knew nothing about it! That's what kills me. *So innocent!* Jenny, I never thought you were like that."

"I'm not like that! It's not what you think." The story sounded worse every minute. "I never guessed it was Brian until a few minutes ago, when I remembered that he raises kittens. He has a girlfriend, so I never thought of him."

"You expect me to believe that? You let me think it's Roger, when all along it was this other guy? How many others are there?"

Steve paced fiercely across the grass, his sneakers making deep impressions in the uncut lawn. Jenny was reminded of that game —Mother May I?—where you take giant steps backward and forward on command. Except in this game, she and Steve were taking giant steps—away from each other.

The thought made Jenny's heart ache.

"I told the truth, Steve," she said softly.

He surveyed her suspiciously, his eyes hooded and wary.

Even angry, how handsome he is, she thought, his hair glinting like spun gold in the late afternoon sunlight, his mouth narrowed to a taut slash.

"You better be straight with me, Jenny, because I don't like being made a fool of. I'm not gonna hang around forever. Make up your mind which one of us you want, but do it fast because I might not be around if you wait too long."

"Don't threaten me, Steve!" Jenny cried. He didn't answer. She saw his set and angry face as he turned away, walked to the back gate and forced it open. Her eyes were too blinded by tears to see him get into his car, but she heard the engine turn over. It started with an angry roar. She listened until it faded into the distance. Make up your mind, it seemed to be saying, but do it fast . . . I might not be around . . . around. . . .

Jenny's legs suddenly folded beneath her. She dropped into a patio chair. Wow, I've really made a mess of everything, she thought. And to top it all, I've lost Steve's trust. In a sense she felt he had a point and that she had even deserved his opinion of her. For she knew that lately, in her most secret fantasies, Brian had played a stellar role. She had not planned it that way—it had just happened.

Now I've really done it, she thought miserably. Steve is hurt, and doesn't trust me at all. But can I blame him?

Sure, she had been sort of disloyal in her heart, because she did like Brian. She'd flirted with him a little, but had checked it before making an idiot out of herself. She felt she could be fairly honest in telling Steve she hadn't led anybody on.

But Steve didn't believe that, and he wouldn't understand her side of the story in a million years. How could she make him see that she was crazy about *him*, and nobody else—that knowing other boys liked her didn't really change that fact? Her daydreams she could dismiss—but was she prepared to lose Steve?

No, she wasn't. But Steve didn't know that. From where he stood, Jenny looked like a cheat. A desperate desire to patch up his opinion of her suddenly consumed her.

But *how*? He probably wouldn't believe her story now.

Engrossed in her own thoughts, Jenny didn't hear her mother step outside.

"Jenny, do you feel like talking?"

Usually, Jenny liked to keep things to herself. Even though she had a pretty open relationship with her parents, she was growing up, and it wasn't a good idea to run to them for everything. But right now, all her mother had to do was put a comforting hand on her shoulder, and Jenny let out her miserable story in a sputtering flood.

Her mother listened, not saying anything until Jenny was finished. "I always thought Steve wasn't quite right for you, Jen. But I also think it's better for you to discover things like that for yourself."

"That's not it, Mom," she protested weakly. Sometimes parents could be so offbase. "I don't think any boy would believe me after this mess. It's not just Steve."

"But you're telling the truth. He ought to recognize that."

But not the whole truth, Jenny thought, guilt twisting inside her. She couldn't tell her mother how she really felt about Brian. It would sound too silly. Besides, it was too personal. She didn't want to share those feelings with anyone.

The kitten clambered clumsily into Jenny's lap, and stood on her hind paws to lick away the tears, which made Jenny giggle. Jenny held her close—a warm bundle of silky fur that had already hollowed out a place in her heart.

"Can we keep her, Mom?" she suddenly remembered to ask.

It had been a while since they'd had a cat. The last one was a gray Manx named Marty, who had been run over in front of the house. They had all been so broken up over it, they'd never replaced him.

"Well, it looks as if she's already made herself at home." Her mother laughed. "She might make a good playmate for old Woolly, and she's going to be a beautiful cat when she grows up." She stroked the tiny, sculptured head. "What'll you name her?"

Immediately, the name "Secret" came to Jenny's mind, but she decided against it.

Steve would go wild if she named the cat that. "I don't know. I can't think of anything."

"Well, something will come to mind." Mrs. Carlson smiled confidently. "Let's go see if we can find her something to eat."

Shiloh Hospital seemed empty without Brian Halsey, at least to Jenny. A new patient, a football player named Bert Jones, took over Brian's old room, but every time Jenny went in to see him she expected to see Brian perched on the bed, grinning.

She even found herself looking for the kind of books Brian would like, in spite of her resolve to not think about him or contact him. She had to consider how Steve would feel if she called Brian, so she didn't, even though she'd told Brian she'd come by sometime. Still, Jenny couldn't stop remembering him, furtively running scenes and words backwards and forwards like a cassette tape.

There was also the kitten—who still didn't have a name—to remind her. Jenny nearly fell off her chair when Brooke suggested the name Secret, too. Secretly, that's how Jenny thought of her.

Shelly had fallen instantly in love with the kitten, but both of them agreed to keep their mouths shut on the subject when Steve was around. Jenny even put the kitten in her room when Steve was expected to come over, just to avoid a scene.

Things just weren't that good between

them. Whenever they were together Jenny felt a fluttery fear in her stomach, scared that she would say or do the wrong thing. Their conversations skirted the awkwardness that loomed between them, as if they were people who hardly knew each other.

Mrs. Durant had left the hospital Thursday. According to the nurses on duty that day, she'd left in all her characteristic splendor. A friend had arrived to do her hair and bring her a freshly pressed coral-pink suit, because, as she explained haughtily, she was not about to be wheeled outside in her bathrobe, even though it was the most exquisite bathrobe worn by anybody in the entire hospital.

Jenny jumped at the chance to do some filing at the nurses' station, because she didn't want her mood to infect the patients. There was nothing worse than a volunteer with a scowl on her face. At least if she were filing, she could pretend the scowl was actually a look of concentration. And today, she didn't think she could muster up much of a smile . . . for anyone.

"Hi, beautiful."

At the sound of the familiar voice, Jenny turned around.

Brian hunched over his crutches, his blue eyes laughing at her. "Hi. So you know who I'm talking to."

"Nothing wrong with knowing what you are." She was pleased to have a comeback.

Lately, she hadn't had the words to express anything at all. But how easy it was to talk to Brian! "How are you doing?" The planes of his cheekbones looked lightly sunburned. To Jenny, he looked fabulous.

"Great. Anything new?" His eyes searched her face.

It was hard not to smile. "Not much. I got a kitten." She lowered her eyes.

"Oh, really?"

Jenny wanted to laugh at how innocent he was trying to appear. How long did he plan to carry out this charade? she wondered.

"Can you take a break and sit outside with me for a minute?"

"Sure." She marked her place in the files and followed him out to the glassed-in patio where patients often sunned themselves.

Today, no one but Brian and Jenny occupied the patio. A miniature Japanese bridge crossed a kidney-shaped goldfish pond, whose surface was covered with lily pads. Lush moss dipped from tiny hills to creep between the cracks in the flagstone path Jenny and Brian walked on.

"Why are you here?" she asked.

"I had to visit my doctor in the building next door."

Jenny laughed. "That's right. Dr. Menkin's office is right down the hall from my father's."

"So how's the kitten?"

"Oh, great. She's Siamese, and likes to play.

She eats so much I think she'll burst, but she just waddles away from her dish."

He chuckled. "With her stomach dragging along the ground. You know where she came from, don't you?" His eyes were such a clear, unmuddied blue that she caught twin reflections of herself in them.

"Yes, I've got a good idea," she whispered breathlessly.

"I confess—I'm your Secret Admirer. I raised that kitten myself—she's one of five in the litter. She was my favorite, I guess, the one with the most definite personality."

"Most likely to succeed?" quipped Jenny.

"Something like that." Brian put his hand over hers. A pleasant current sped up her arm.

"Did you raise the flowers, too?"

"The what? Oh, the flowers?" He grinned. "No."

He grew quiet, and the only sounds were from the distant intercom in the building and the gentle *plop-plop* of goldfish in the pond.

"I wanted to see you again, and I sorta thought you'd stop by." Absently, he twirled the amethyst pinky ring Jenny wore on her little finger. Thad had bought it last year for her birthday.

"I-I was going to, Brian, but . . ." Was it the right time to tell him about Steve? If she did that, there would be no turning back. But she had to, she was *Steve's girl;* and she couldn't keep Brian on false hopes.

"Why didn't you?"

"I have a boyfriend and he, well, he . . . I'm still going with him." Jenny felt, rather than saw, Brian's hand slip off her own.

"Oh."

"He got really upset about the Secret Admirer gifts, so I couldn't . . ." It sounded so lame, like a dumb, weak excuse, she thought, feeling slightly sick.

"I kinda thought it was something like that. I mean, somebody like you would be sure to have a guy, right?"

"Not necessarily."

"I knew you went to the dance with him." Brian tried to smile, but it came out crooked. "I saw you with him at the hospital."

"Look, I really care about you. I loved the Secret Admirer gifts." The question burned on her lips, and since they might not see each other anymore, she went ahead and asked, "Why, *me*, though? I thought you already had a girlfriend?"

Brian gazed into the pond, his face reflected darkly between two lily pads. "Elaine and I used to date last year, but we don't anymore. We're just friends."

"Thank you," Jenny whispered, her heart so full she thought she'd start crying.

"Maybe Elaine and I will start going out again, I don't know." He shrugged.

Jenny hoped her disappointment didn't show, but what could she expect of him? To wait for her and Steve to split up?

Brian's gaze settled on hers. "Hey, what did you name the kitty?"

"I call her 'Secret,'" she confided. It was okay to tell Brian.

"Secret is perfect for her. Wait till she grows up—she'll be beautiful. You'll have to see her mom, Tai-Lu . . . someday."

"Yeah, I'd like that." But as the words left Jenny's lips, she knew that would probably never happen.

"Look, Jenny. If you break up with what's-his-name, I'm still around, okay? But until then." He leaned forward and kissed her cheek lightly. The scent of his cologne wafted over her. "I guess it's goodbye."

"I guess so," Jenny mumbled.

Brian hooked his crutches under his arms and started to hop away. "And take care of Secret, okay?"

"I will."

Jenny held the glass door open to let him pass, then watched him hop-walk down the long hospital corridor until he was out of sight.

Gone forever, she thought, forcing back tears.

If only I could have him, she thought, lying awake in the darkness. It was strange how she could gain boys' attention whom she wasn't interested in without really trying—Skip and Roger both had invited her out again, but she declined. She didn't like either for anything other than friends, and she didn't want to give them any other ideas. She knew in her heart that she wasn't facing up to the fact she wanted out of the relationship with Steve. And she wasn't facing the fact that she was crazy about Brian. If she didn't know how she felt in any other way, she could tell by how her chest tightened up at the thought of Steve, and how light and joyful she felt at the thought of Brian. Unbidden pictures of him flashed into her mind; the way he smoothed back his hair, how he smiled. Even how he hobbled on his crutches had become a bittersweet memory to her.

Jenny met Shelly at Wellington's after school.

"Jay and I are going to the zoo this weekend. Doesn't that sound like fun? I'm just so happy with him. We do such neat things together," she added.

"I think Steve is taking me to a surf movie," Jenny informed her lifelessly.

"You used to get excited about surf movies. What happened? Don't you like Steve anymore?" Shelly's gaze probed her, and Jenny felt like shrinking from her inquisitiveness.

She simply shrugged. "They're okay, but you've seen one you've seen them all. That is, unless you're an addict, like Steve."

"It's his 'thing,' Jenny. How many volleyball games has he attended, just for the record?"

"Not as many as I've seen surf movies." Jenny laughed, remembering Steve's appraisal of Evan at the championship game. "You know you can tell how old the films are by the style of the swimming trunks."

Shelly chuckled. "I never thought of that, but it's true. By the way, how's Brian doing? Have you heard from him?"

Only in my dreams, Jenny felt like saying, but refrained. "Uh, no," she lied, she didn't want to admit to Shelly she had seen Brian at the hospital.

Shelly looked at her strangely, but why wouldn't she? Jenny thought. She has no way of knowing about Brian, unless she saw him herself. It was better not to confide in her best friend at this point, and risk Steve thinking she was Ms. Popularity or some boy-crazy nitwit.

"What about Skip or Roger? Have they called?"

"Yes. They both asked me out." Jenny smiled. "But I said no to them. No need adding fuel to the fire."

"No. I understand Roger is a good bowling date, if you like to lose." They both laughed. "Next weekend Jay's taking me to a volleyball tourney over in San Jose. College teams."

"Sounds like fun. Would you mind a third wheel?"

"We'll see." Shelly winked at her conspiratorially. "You might have a better offer before then."

"Ha ha. If it's another surf movie, I think I'll go with you, if you don't mind."

"The more the noisier," Shelly said expansively. Jenny could not help thinking that Shelly was the loudest of the three.

Shelly finished her hot fudge sundae and was looking around greedily. "I could do with another scoop," she said.

"I hate to ask, but how's the diet going?" Jenny grinned, as she watched Shelly's face fall.

"Must you mention it! Trying not to eat is like trying not to breathe. This will be my dinner, by the way."

"Is this Shelly's Fast Weight Loss Campaign?" Jenny eyed her critically, knowing her friend's penchant for weight-loss books and crazy crash programs.

"This is my Spur-of-the-Moment Hot Fudge Sundae Program." Shelly giggled. She sipped her water. "Now if you have your jogging shoes on, we can run home, thereby dropping a few pounds."

"You have to run at least five miles to drop one pound, I think," Jenny reminded her.

"Let's get going, then. We've only got an hour before dark." Shelly paid the bill and they sprinted lightly out of Wellington's.

"Your practice runs with Evan sure make you a tough act to follow," Shelly said as she puffed along behind Jenny.

"He keeps me in shape, although I'm not nearly as fast as he is. He has great stamina,

140

too." Jenny kept a steady pace ahead of her friend, thinking of how Evan would enjoy meeting Brian. They shared so much in common. Evan was the high school's star track man this season.

As they rounded the corner, Jenny spied Steve's car parked in the driveway of his house.

Her heart caught in her throat, and she felt a little queasy.

"There's Steve."

Shelly trudged up beside her. "So? He doesn't bite, does he?"

Jenny hadn't really wanted to see him, but he had already spotted her and was waving. Reluctantly, she waved back and ran towards him.

"You look healthy," he remarked as she skipped onto the driveway. "Is this how you keep in such good form for volleyball?"

"It's part of it," she said; her voice sounded unnatural to her own ear. She watched him pull out some spark plugs. "Car problem?" she inquired.

"Hmmm. It's having trouble starting." He buried his head back underneath the hood.

"If you can't fix it, we might be able to take my father's car," Jenny offered.

"Yeah, thanks," his answer came out muffled. "I'm pretty sure I can figure it out."

"I'll see you later, then." Jenny wondered when it had become so difficult to talk to him. Just today? When had she noticed it? Or had it been happening all the time, she just hadn't been aware of it until now?

She couldn't remember if he said goodbye or not. Somehow it didn't seem important. When she got into Shelly's car and shut the door behind her, Steve didn't even look up and wave.

"You won't believe who the Secret Admirer is, Evan." Jenny dropped a Mendelssohn album on the turntable and turned up the volume, filling Evan's room with music.

"Try me."

Evan's room was done in browns. Sports pennants hung above the bed, a row of track trophies sat on the bookshelf, where Evan used a pair of battered Adidas as bookends.

Gazing at them, Jenny said, "Did I tell you Brian was a track champ?"

"Is his name by any chance Brian Halsey?"

"Yes. How'd you know?"

"I don't know why I didn't put two and two together before now. But anyone who's into track knows Brian Halsey's name. He's famous around these parts."

"Is that so?" Jenny smiled to herself.

"What is that smile all about?" Evan flopped down in the rocker across from her.

"Brian Halsey, famous track star, is my Secret Admirer."

"No kidding?" Evan sounded astonished. "He gave you the kitten, the flowers, the letters?"

"Yes, Evan," Jenny said patiently.

"Aren't you happy?"

"Sort of, except that it's too late for me to get involved with him. I'm still seeing Steve, and besides, he's going out with Elaine again."

"This is beginning to sound like a modern-day version of Romeo and Juliet. Star-crossed love. The story gets richer, more invlolved as time goes on," Evan said, his foot tapping out the beat of Mendelssohn.

"Don't make fun of me." Jenny's voice quavered.

"Does Shelly know all this yet?"

"I haven't told her about Brian because I was afraid she might tell her brother."

"She does have a problem that way. Lovable, but definitely a big mouth," Evan agreed, patting Jenny's shoulder affectionately. "I'm glad you considered me friend enough to confide in me."

"I'm glad you're here."

Evan took the record off the turntable and switched off the stereo. "Come on. Let's go for a run. We can talk between breaths."

"I don't have the energy," Jenny said.

"Sure you do," Evan insisted.

Once they were on the path, Evan said, "You realize, don't you, that Halsey is a better runner than I am? He's going to leave you in the dust."

"Maybe not. Remember, he broke his leg. He has to let it heal, and by the time it gets better, I could be as good as he is." Jenny laughed. "Anyway, what makes you think I'll ever run with him?"

Evan didn't answer but instead ran ahead of her into the woods.

"Evan, where are you? Come on, don't tease me, you goon," Jenny called. Tears streaked down her face. No matter what she did lately, she found herself crying at the most inopportune moments.

When they got to the pond, Evan turned and saw her tear-streaked face. "Look, Jenny. If you're going to cry every time I turn around, I'm not taking you anywhere anymore."

She tried to laugh.

"It's ridiculous. If Steve is making you this unhappy . . ."

She cut him off. "Steve has nothing to do with it . . ."

"Steve has a lot to do with it. I'm not blind. Steve is the source of a lot of your misery. You two just aren't meant for each other, that's all. No big deal. You are moving in separate directions. Face it, kiddo."

"No," Jenny stated stubbornly.

"All right. Be that way. But sooner or later, it's going to happen whether you like it or not. You're going to break up. It's inevitable. He knows it and you know it. I bet even dingy Shelly knows it. Doesn't your mother know it?"

Evan could be a pain sometimes. "My mother has never liked Steve, you know that. She has biased opinions."

"She knows he makes you unhappy. People who know you well will always be able to pick out things like that. So it pays to listen to family and friends." Evan was so logical it was making Jenny sick.

"Do you always listen to yours?" she shot back. "How about when you fell in love with Wanda Ellingsworth, and she left you for the guitar picker from Arizona? You didn't listen to anyone then."

"No, you're right. How do you think I learned all this stuff? The hard way—just like you. My mother said she was wrong for me, and you kept asking me what I was doing with her, but I just couldn't see it."

Jenny laughed.

"But sometimes, you have to live and learn —and you've got to admit there was something about her—"

"The guitar picker apparently agreed with you," Jenny could not resist saying.

"Did he ever!" Evan let out a short laugh. "And did I suffer for it! And d'you know? She didn't even like classical music. Now how could I possibly get involved with a girl who didn't like my most important love?"

"It would never have lasted," Jenny said with conviction.

"And the same is true of you and Steve," Evan said firmly, covering her hand with his.

"I'm not ready for it, Evan." Jenny wanted to lean on his shoulder and cry.

"It's going to happen whether you are ready

or not. Remember the old tag game, 'coming— ready or not'?" He chuckled. "That's how it is. Trust me."

"I don't even want to listen to you." She covered her ears with her hands.

He pried her hands off her ears. "You once told me I was the most honest person you knew. You know I'm right."

She scrambled to her feet, fighting back a new onslaught of tears. "Come on. I need the practice. Let's run around the pond, then back up by the pumpkin farm."

"If you're going to try to keep up with Halsey, you will need the practice," Evan reminded her.

Jenny yanked playfully on his sweatshirt. "I'm not going to even try!" Already she felt more cheerful. Perhaps things would work out. It was good to have a friend like Evan.

10

A boy with sun-bleached hair balanced himself precariously at the end of his surfboard, arms outstretched, feet positioned expertly as the board skimmed along the inner coil of wave. Just like Steve, Jenny thought, as the film crackled, end-of-the-reel numbers flitted past, and the next scene showed the boy paddling to shore, muscular, tanned arms plowing through the water.

Wolf-whistles and clapping thundered through the tiny theater as the lights popped on for intermission. Everybody there looked pleased and excited by the movie . . . except Jenny.

It was a great sport for those who were involved with it, but she could see clearly now that she wasn't a true lover of surfing. All along, her only interest in it had been watching Steve, listening to Steve, wanting to share with Steve as best she knew how.

There were many girls in the audience, too—really good surfers who could genuinely share the sport with their boyfriends. Jenny knew some, like Lindsay Farmer who was in Art class. Lindsay said she got up every morning before school to go surfing. Now that was dedication.

Instead of turning to Jenny to talk, Steve swiveled in his seat to talk to the boy on his opposite side. Your basic surfer type, Jenny thought irritably. What was there to talk about? They'd just sat through two surf movies that were incredibly alike. How many times did you have to watch a guy ride a wave before you were totally bored?

Well, obviously, she was about the only one who was bored. Everyone wandered around, talking to each other. Jenny stood at Steve's side, but she might as well have been invisible for all he cared.

"You fix up that board, yet, Fleming?"

"Naw—I'll have it out next week, though."

"I'm pretty stoked about my new board. It's a Haut."

"I heard. I'll be over. How're the waves at Mitchells?"

And on it went. Jenny broke away, knowing she wouldn't be missed, to buy herself a Coke. She felt really out of place, like a rose in a turnip patch.

She wandered back to Steve, who was still talking.

"Oh, there you are. I guess we better go. Good movie, huh?"

"Great, Steve."

"No need to get sarcastic, Jenny. You knew what these movies are like," he snapped.

"I guess I've seen too many of them," she returned, unable to shake that terrible, let-down feeling.

"Wow, sorry," he said, looking hurt.

Jenny sensed the prickliness between them, but she couldn't stop her part of it. Anything and everything she said rubbed him the wrong way, and vice versa. *What happened to the way we used to be*? she asked herself, climbing into the passenger seat of Steve's Toyota.

"It's not your fault, Steve," she amended wearily.

"Next time I'll just go with my friends, okay?" He gunned the motor savagely.

"I'm sorry, I guess I just can't share surfing with you. Surfers are just so . . . dedicated."

"What's wrong with that? You're always saying how dedicated some doctors are."

"Being a doctor is different."

"Oh? Being a surfer isn't as good, huh?"

"I didn't say that! It's not a profession . . . it's not saving lives." How snooty she sounded . . . but she hadn't meant it to come out that way. Still, there was no taking back those words. Steve was off and running with them now.

"Well, maybe I'd like to surf professionally some day. Did you ever think of that?"

"I didn't know you were even thinking of that." Jenny felt awful. "I didn't really mean it how it sounded."

Steve pounded his fist against the steering wheel. "I don't know what's gotten into you, Jenny, but you're different. Maybe it was that guy at the hospital . . . all this stuff happening . . . I just don't know." He gulped, and his Adam's apple, silhouetted against the night, jumped up and down. "I can't talk to you anymore."

"You can talk to me all you want, Steve," she returned, unable to check the bitterness rising in her voice. "You just *ignored* me the whole evening. And I don't think you even noticed."

"You ignore me when you're studying," he shot back. "When you're thinking about your volunteer work, you're not thinking about me."

Suddenly, Jenny knew that she'd been forcing herself into a mold to suit Steve for quite a while now. But the real Jenny was screaming to get out. It wasn't Steve's fault. Maybe it was more hers, for thinking it was possible in the first place.

What was it her dad had said the other day? "You're changing, Jenny. You've grown up so much just since you started working at the hospital. I see a whole new person in you."

Was that what Steve saw, too? Was that what he didn't like—or had he changed, too, in a different way?

Jenny was sure she would burst into tears if

she sat next to him a minute longer. She opened the car door, and scooted out.

"Steve, thanks for taking me," she told him in a fierce whisper.

He looked straight ahead, his profile etched against the honeysuckle—not turning to look at her one last time before driving off. "Goodbye, Jenny," he said.

Jenny whirled around and ran across the gravel.

"Jenny, are you all right?" Dr. Carlson was alarmed at the sound of his oldest daughter padding quickly to her room—without so much as a hello to the rest of the family.

Jenny held her hands over her face, unable to offer even a strangled yes. Why can't they forget I exist, just for tonight, and let me get through this? she wished bitterly.

Tears coursed down her face unchecked. There was no way in the world she could stop them. They leaked out the corners of her eyes and soaked into her yellow bedspread, and when she looked at her swollen face in the mirror, they spilled onto the polished mahogany dresser.

I'm going to cry forever, Jenny thought miserably.

"Why are you crying?" Brooke stood in the doorway, studying her with curiosity. "You never cry."

"Go away, Brooke. Just let me alone, okay?"

Brooke sat down on the edge of the bed.

"But you must be really upset, Jen. Did you and Steve have a fight?"

"Sort of. Now just go, please."

Her father filled the doorframe. "Jenny, what's wrong? I've never seen you so upset." His strong arms wrapped around her quaking shoulders, quieting her a little.

Jenny felt comforted from the outside, but it didn't help deep down where the tears seemed to keep coming from—some hidden well-spring she'd never known existed.

"Is breaking up with somebody always this hard?" she choked out finally, after the first wave of sobs had passed.

"It's never been easy, Jen." Dr. Carlson smiled warmly. "Why do you think there are so many songs written about it?"

"I'm never going to go through this again!"

"You say that now, but you'll change your mind. Someone will come along who'll seem special to you, and you'll forget about Steve by then."

Someone already has. But even the memory of Brian couldn't make her forget Steve. She would never forget Steve, and right now, that loss filled her. What she and Steve had had together was gone forever.

"He was my first boyfriend," Jenny mumbled into her pillow.

"I know, but he won't be your last. You're an intelligent, pretty girl, and you've got your whole life ahead of you.

"I've told you that you've changed, and I don't think you see it yet, but you will in time,

Jen. Nothing stays the same forever," her father told her.

"Nothing?" The thought horrified her. What if she went through life like this, up and down, falling in love and suffering this agony at the end . . . ?

"Well, some things, but you've got to be prepared for changes, and welcome them." He handed her a Kleenex and lowered himself into the rocking chair, which was much too small for him.

Jenny sighed heavily. Her chest ached from crying so hard.

"I never counted on this happening," she said.

"No one ever does."

"Where's Mom?"

"At an auxiliary meeting. She'll be home soon."

"She's going to say 'I told you so,'" Jenny said. "She always thought Steve and I weren't right for each other."

"No, she won't, Jenny. Your mother understands. When I was your age, Jen, I had a girlfriend who was very special. We did everything together—we even planned to go to the same college. But what we didn't plan on was what course our emotions would take. A year later, we were two different people, and even though it was sad, we drifted apart." Dr. Carlson smiled in a way Jenny had seen before, his "good old days," smile, she called it.

"What happened to her? Did you ever see her again?" Brooke wanted to know. The idea

153

of her dad having an old girlfriend was interesting to her.

He shrugged. "Oh, I saw her now and then at holidays. Her name was Lucy. But don't mention her name to your mother. She turns green around the ears."

"*Lucy!*" Brooke shrieked with delight. "I wonder what she looks like now."

"Who knows—she probably has teenagers of her own," her dad said.

"Wait till I tell my friends!"

"Wait till you get a boyfriend, Brooke." Dr. Carlson's eyes gleamed. "You'll see."

Brooke put her hands on her hips and shook her head in determination. "Not me, Dad. I'm never going to fall in love. *Never!*"

Jenny and her dad exchanged glances.

"Sure, Brookie." Jenny grinned. "Famous last words."

"Okay, tell me everything, from beginning to end."

Shelly sat cross-legged on Jenny's bed, eager to hear every detail of last night's argument.

Jenny slumped in her rocking chair, legs dangling over one curved arm. Her heart felt like it was tied to a lead weight as she related the whole story.

Telling Shelly only made her feel worse, because as she repeated what she and Steve had said to each other, those words imprinted themselves in her mind with painful clarity.

"So, I guess you and Steve are quits, now, huh?" Shelly smiled sympathetically.

"Yeah, you could say that." Jenny sighed. "But I really wish we could stay friends. I mean, that part's awful, Shelly. He's my best friend's brother. When I go over to your house, I've got to face him. How am I going to do that? I liked it better when we hardly knew each other, last year."

"I see what you mean. But just ignore him. Say 'hi' like you never knew each other very well."

"Oh, sure. That's easy for you to say." Absently, Jenny twisted a lock of blond hair around her finger.

"You know he's gonna feel just as weird as you do, Jen," Shelly said. "He probably feels lousy about the surf movie, too. By now, he realizes he acted like a flake and maybe he wants to make up."

"I doubt it. The way it was between us . . . I don't know if I . . ." She stopped herself. It was the closest she'd ever come to admitting that she didn't really want Steve back, wasn't it? What *do* I want then, she asked herself, if I don't want Steve? Have I outgrown him, the way Mom and Dad think?

It sure didn't feel like it—ever since last night, Jenny was lonelier and emptier than she'd ever been in her whole life.

Shelly finished the thought aloud. "You don't know if you want him back, huh? I suspected as much. I always did wonder what you saw in him, but maybe that's just because he's my brother."

"I'm sure that has a lot to do with it." Jenny chuckled.

"Well, now that you know the Secret Admirer is none other than that hunk, Brian Halsey, what are you going to do about it?" Shelly's eyes lit up in anticipation.

"Hey, come on, Shelly!"

"Listen." Her friend's voice dropped to a hushed whisper, as if she were sharing a big secret. "I just *knew*, when you made those extra trips to Shiloh, that you weren't going to see your dad. You never visited him that much before, unless he needed office work done. Once, before the kitten came, Jay mentioned how Brian liked you, but I didn't tell you. Imagine me—not saying anything! So it wasn't all that hard to put two and two together."

"Brilliant deduction, Shelly." Jenny frowned, but she really didn't care anymore. It was over with Brian—and Steve. What difference did it make if Shelly wanted to blab to the whole world?

"So what are you going to do about Brian?" Shelly persisted.

"Nothing."

"*Nothing?*" Shelly was aghast. "What's the matter with you? He's crazy about you! If a guy gave me a Siamese kitten and all those things, I'd fall right into his arms."

"You don't understand, Shelly. I'm not

ready to get involved with someone else right now. I need to get my head on straight. Besides," she added, "Steve thinks I led Brian and Roger on, but I never did. Honest. You know how long I've known Roger, and I just visited Brian because he asked me to. But I had no idea how he felt about me until the other day."

"Little Ms. Good Samaritan, huh?" Shelly grinned mischievously. "And Steve just decided to make a federal case out of it."

"Sort of." Jenny traced her fingernail along the stitching of her jeans. "And the last thing I want Steve to think is that he was right—the minute we break up I run off with someone else."

"Yeah, I see what you mean. But I still think you're crazy."

"You know what Steve will think, and I don't want Brian to think that, either."

Just then, the kitten crawled sleepily out of her basket, stretched and trotted over to Jenny, who scooped her up.

"Oooh, you're adorable," Shelly cooed, reaching for her. "Did you name her yet?"

"Secret . . . what else?"

Shelly laughed. "Did you tell Steve?"

"Are you kidding?" Jenny smiled. "The name fit when she arrived, but I was scared to name her in case Steve got upset. But what else could I call her?"

"Right. It's perfect."

Shelly pulled a ribbon from her hair for the kitten to chase across the bedspread.

"Hey, don't do that, she'll get her claws in the spread."

"Sorry," she said distractedly. "I don't know how you put up with those surf movies as long as you did. I sure wouldn't. I'm glad Jay isn't into that stuff. At least Jay and I have something in common. I'm going to be the next Barbara Walters and he's going to be Walter Cronkite."

"The news team of the future, huh?" Jenny said, feeling better than she had in a long time.

"Jenny, are you going to mope around this house forever?" Mrs. Carlson asked, finding her daughter curled up on her bed, reading.

"I'm not moping, Mom. I'm reading," Jenny returned. "Since when was reading called moping?"

"Since you broke up with Steve," her mother replied candidly. "You really spend too much time in your room. I don't mean to pry, but you should go out. Aren't there any other nice boys you could date? I'm sure there are."

"Mom, please. You are prying." Jenny sighed, feeling invaded. Didn't Mom remember that she hadn't ever spent lots of time with Steve, so why was she making such a big deal about the empty slots in Jenny's life right now?

Especially annoying was when Saturday night rolled around, and she didn't have a date. Mom and Dad gave her those big, mournful-eyed looks that made her wish she could do something just to make *them* feel better about her not going out. It was weird how her parents could get so tied up in her happiness, as if they were somehow responsible for it at all times.

Luckily, last weekend, Jay had to go out of town with his folks, so Jenny and Shelly had gone roller skating, which was fun. They went to the beach on Sunday to watch a volleyball tournament, then came home and did homework together.

But naturally, par for the course, her mother just had to ask, "Did you meet any nice boys there?"

Shelly whooped with laughter, running down a description of some of the male players, while Jenny sat there, silently screaming.

But what no one knew was that several times she had stood next to the phone, ready to dial Brian's number. It would be so good to hear his voice, hear it slide gently over the syllables in her name. . . .

Why didn't she? Because, Jenny was quick to remind herself, Elaine might be going out with Brian now. And she didn't want to risk her heart to Brian if he wasn't interested anymore. Maybe the two of them would never get together, but it was better that way than starting out all wrong, she figured.

"I know Bill Thompson down at the U-Save Market would like to see more of you." Her mother cut into Jenny's thoughts. "Why don't you make an appearance down there? You know he's working part-time to help with his college tuition."

"I don't want to. Thanks anyway, Mom," Jenny replied. She wished her mother wouldn't try to matchmake for her.

Later, Bill Thompson just happened to come by with an order of groceries for Mrs. Carlson. Against her will, Jenny was summoned to put the groceries away—and to meet Bill.

"Nice to meet you," Jenny said, shaking hands. The pink tinge on Bill's ears denoted that he was just as embarrassed about this introduction as she was.

Both Jenny and Bill seemed relieved when he was allowed to leave, even though it was pouring rain outside. And poor Bill had already looked like a drowned rat when he arrived at the house.

"Isn't he a nice boy, Jen?" her mom twittered, unpacking the food.

"Yes, Mom. He's a nice boy," Jenny mimicked, and they both started laughing. "I don't need a matchmaker, Mom. I'm fine, really."

A stiff wind flung raindrops at Jenny's bedroom window. The power dimmed, then came on again. It was the perfect day to be reading a brooding, Gothic romance, Shelly would say. Jenny was reading *Hamlet* for English class, which was brooding enough, she considered, curling up against the Miss Piggy Steve had won for her at the Boardwalk.

I'll always remember him, Jenny thought

wistfully, her heart taking a sudden turn. She extracted Secret's claws from Miss Piggy's frilly pink dress. Steve's picture stared back at her from the dresser top, where she'd placed it on a lace doily. He looked more mature to her in the photo than he did in real life.

It was funny that she always thought of Steve as being younger than Brian, yet the reverse was true. Age really had nothing to do with anything, did it?

In fact, when she broke it down, there was nothing Jenny could pinpoint that made she and Steve so abruptly incompatible. They'd just changed, and neither of them was wrong. It just happened. Her mother had said that you change so much in your teen years, that by the time you turn twenty you hardly recognize the person you were at fifteen.

Could that be true? Jenny felt like she'd stay this way forever—and yet, here she was, falling out of love, going through changes which sent her emotions screaming up and down like a roller coaster. And she hated roller coasters!

At school, Jenny hardly ever saw Steve, where before they both made a point of walking to some of their classes together. They used to meet for lunch, and after school. Now they avoided each other, making up new routes so that they didn't even have to say "hi." Even "hi" was awkward.

Even worse, Jenny didn't go over to Shelly's anymore. Shelly came to her house. It just wasn't worth the risk of running into Steve and feeling bad all over again.

Sighing, she laid *Hamlet* down and opened her desk drawer. There were several mementos of dates with Steve: movie ticket stubs, the program for a high school play Steve had performed in, *The Lion, the Witch and the Wardrobe,* a valentine, a photo of the two of them at the beach, sticking their tongues out at the camera, a silver dollar he'd given her— all mixed together with the Secret Admirer messages.

Jenny located an old shoe box, gathered up the memorabilia and dropped it carefully inside. On top, she laid the framed photograph of Steve. Secret pounced in clumsily.

"No, you can't go," Jenny said, lifting her out.

She secured the box with a rubber band and put it on a shelf at the top of her closet.

Maybe when I'm twenty, she thought, I'll open that box again.

11

On Saturday morning, Jenny was getting ready to accompany her dad to his office to do some typing and filing. His secretary was on vacation, and he was desperate for help.

When the phone rang, Jenny didn't pay much attention to it. Her parents and Brooke seemed to be most in demand lately. If it was for her, it was either Shelly or Angie Morgan, with whom she'd become friends. And this morning, she didn't have time to linger on the phone for very long.

"Jenny, it's for you." Her mother winked at her father.

"Remember me? Brian Halsey here, recovering nicely from an auto accident . . . let's see, about four weeks ago?"

"Brian!" Forgetting herself completely, Jenny started laughing. Tears filled her eyes. "It's good to hear from you!"

"Likewise. Listen, I didn't want to intrude, you know. After I saw you last . . . I realize you have a boyfriend and I—"

"Not anymore," she cut him off. "I don't have a boyfriend right now."

"Oh? Does that mean this is my lucky day or what?"

Jenny giggled. "It could be. How are you doing?"

"Oh, great, just great." He sounded distracted. "So you're free now, huh? When you didn't call, I figured you were still going with someone, so I better just bug off. . . ."

"Yeah, well. It didn't work out," Jenny admitted softly.

"Why didn't you call?"

"It didn't seem right, Brian. I needed some space to . . . to think. It's kind of hard to explain over the phone," she replied, feeling awkward with her whole family listening.

Brooke passed by, fluttering her eyelashes and giggling. Mom and Dad exchanged meaningful glances. Thad was the only one minding his own business, chomping on his cereal.

"Can we get together and talk? My folks . . . I mean, my family is taking the boat out tomorrow. Maybe you can come with us? We'll sail over to Moss Landing and have lunch. Do you like seafood?"

"Love it."

"Good. See you then."

"'Bye." Jenny turned to find everyone

watching her expectantly. "Can't I ever have a private phone conversation?" she grumbled, but her heart was soaring.

Brian looked even better than Jenny had remembered. Still on crutches but looking more at ease with them, he seemed taller. His face and arms were lightly tanned, but his eyes were the same stunning blue that Jenny had not been able to forget.

Secret purred appreciatively as Brian stroked her. Laughing, he pronounced, "Dr. Brian says you're a winner, Secret." To which she uttered a strictly Siamese meow as she was lowered to the floor.

As if it were the most natural thing in the world, Brian took Jenny's hand when they got in the car. "I've been exercising and doing therapy," he told her. "Dr. Menkin says I'll be running circles around everyone pretty soon, which I'm real glad about. There's one more operation to go, though."

"Oh, Brian, no."

"Oh, yes. I've gotta have the pins removed, remember?"

The thought of him going back into hospital saddened Jenny, but she knew he would weather it as he did everything else—with spirit.

Brian's mother did the driving. Jenny noticed that Brian called his father by his first name, Max, instead of "Dad." A lot of kids did that. Later, while the adults were busy in the boat and she and Brian stood on the slip waiting to come aboard, Brian explained the situation.

"Max isn't my real dad, if you didn't guess already. My mom's marrying him pretty soon. He's a really nice guy. You'll see."

Max was an attractive match for the pretty, chestnut-haired Mrs. Halsey. He had a pleasant, narrow face filled out by a full beard and mustache, and blue-black hair.

His boat was a twenty-footer, according to Brian, gleaming white with a bold red, white and blue striped sail that bulged with wind once they reached open sea. Jenny knew nothing about sailing, and had only been on motorboats before. But she found that she loved the feel of the sailboat dependent on the wind, how it dipped and leaned as it cut through the waves.

"I could get addicted to this," she told Brian.

They sat huddled together on a middle seat.

"I told you you'd like it." The wind blew Brian's hair into a mass of tight ringlets. "I'm gonna learn to sail this boat myself, as soon as I get back on my feet. Max says he'll teach me, isn't that right, Max?"

"Only when it's safe to throw your crutches overboard, mate," Max said good-naturedly, dropping his white seaman's cap onto Brian's tousled hair. "That cast is an anchor."

Jenny glanced at the white lump protruding from Brian's jeans and thought of how funny and pale his leg would look when it came off.

The cast was covered with scribbles all the way to the toe, reminding her that she still hadn't signed it.

Brian pulled the cap down over his brow and surveyed her with amusement. "I don't have your autograph here, do I, miss?" he asked, clumping the cast down next to her.

"There's no room," she said, but he pulled up his pants leg a little.

"Here . . . right in front. I saved you a place."

She wrote: *To Brian, with love, Jenny.*

The pier at Moss Landing appeared out of a light fog, a tiny Tinkertoy creation overshadowed by the factory smokestacks rising behind it. The area looked altogether different from the sea.

"We're eating at Marco's. Ever been there?" Max asked Jenny.

"No. I've never heard of it."

"Once you've eaten there, you'll never forget it," Brian said. "Catch of the day, artichoke soup and french-fried artichokes . . . mmm, I can't wait. They even make their own bread."

"Stop! I don't want to hear anymore." Jenny laughed.

Once the sailboat was secured, they walked along the pier to Marco's, a whitewashed shanty with faded blue curtains and a neon sign on top. It didn't look inviting, Jenny thought.

"Just goes to prove that looks are deceiving," Brian said a few minutes later, reading

Jenny's expression. "I know I asked you if you liked seafood, but have you ever had artichoke soup? It's really good."

"No, but I like artichokes." Jenny scanned the menu and found the soup, served with fresh bread and salad. "I'll try it."

Brian ordered the same for himself. They were seated in a corner booth overlooking the harbor, while Max and Brian's mother were having a drink at the bar.

"I'm glad you could come today," Brian said.

"Me, too."

"I thought you might not want to."

"Really?"

He blushed. "Well, you know, in light of all that's happened. I'm glad you're not going with what's-his-name anymore."

She started to say Steve's name, but he knew what she was going to say and he put his finger over her mouth.

"No, I don't want to know who he is. I just want to know you."

Jenny couldn't believe this was happening. If she pinched herself, maybe she'd wake up and find she wasn't here at all. Brian's hand slid into hers, and he looked at her fingers thoughtfully.

"Do you read palms?" she asked jokingly.

"What? No." He smiled. "Just thinking . . . about us. Can there be an 'us' now?"

"I'd like that, Brian."

"Yeah, but are you all done thinking? I mean, do you have what's-his-name completely out of your system? It isn't my style to get in the way, if you know what I mean."

Candlelight danced along the planes of his face, and Jenny had an urge to reach out and smooth his rumpled hair from his forehead.

"That's why I didn't call you before," Jenny tried to explain. "Because I wanted to make sure of how I felt about everything. I didn't want you to think I chose you on the rebound, or have any doubts in myself."

"If he asked you to go back, would you go?"

Had he been worrying about that all along? "No." She was quiet for a moment. "I was afraid to get involved with anyone again . . . especially after you told me about Elaine."

He grinned. "Elaine's not my old girlfriend —she's my cousin. I just told you that to throw you off. It worked, didn't it?" Seeing her stunned look, he added, "Maybe I shouldn't have done that, but I didn't want you to know how much you mattered to me. Are you ready to take your chances?"

"I think so."

Their order arrived. Brian carved thick slices of the homemade bread for both of them. One whiff of the fragrant soup made Jenny realize how hungry she really was.

But she couldn't compete with Brian, who ordered a second bowl of soup. "Max brings us over here about every other week, if the weather's nice," he explained. "But I never get enough of this soup. I'm gonna learn to make it."

"Isn't it easier to buy a week's supply? Stripping artichoke leaves is a hassle."

"I guess you're right." He offered her another slice of bread. "My father's a gourmet cook, though, so nothing is too much to tackle for him. He knows an easy way to do all that stuff."

"Does he live near you?" Jenny didn't want to sound too curious about his family, even though she was.

"No. He moved to Washington after the divorce. He's starting a big chain of restaurants, and writing a gourmet cookbook. I see him on holidays. My younger brother, Tim, and I go up there at Christmas, and we write. It's not so bad—we've done that for two years now."

"How old is your brother?"

"Nine. He's at a soccer roundup this weekend."

Jenny had all but forgotten about Max and Mrs. Halsey, who appeared at their table. Suddenly she realized the couple had purposely eaten at another table so that she and Brian could spend some time alone together.

"Have a nice lunch, you two?" Max couldn't keep a teasing note out of his voice.

Jenny turned red, but Brian seemed nonplussed. "Great, just great, Max, thanks. Best lunch I've ever had."

The four of them strolled along the piers, laughing and talking. Jenny felt right at home with Mrs. Halsey and Brian's step-father-to-be. She wondered why the Halseys had gotten a divorce in the first place, but figured it wasn't any of her business, and Brian hadn't offered that information. She knew that people got divorced for reasons other people on the outside couldn't always understand. Sort of like Jenny and Steve. . . .

Brian helped Jenny back on board the *Hetty Mae*, which Max had fondly named his boat. "Hetty's my grandma's name, and Mae's my favorite sister," he explained.

Max started the outboard motor that would get them out of the harbor, and then set sail for home.

Jenny and Brian settled into their seat, and while the adults were occupied at the helm, Brian leaned over and kissed her. His lips felt cold and tasted salty, but they warmed quickly, sending pleasant thrills along Jenny's spine. Droplets of sea spray slid from Brian's hair onto her nose.

"I've missed you, Jenny," he whispered, his blue eyes penetrating her own. Everything about Brian was so startlingly alive. Jenny felt she would remember him forever against today's cloudless, cobalt sky—as if her mind held a snapshot of that very scene.

"Me, too," she responded softly as he folded her in his embrace.

He kissed the fine salt spray from her face, and Jenny was torn between closing her eyes and concentrating on his touch, or keeping them open so she didn't miss a blink of his long, dark lashes.

It was as though they were the only two

people in the world, sailing off to some un-charted island—just the two of them. Again, she completely forgot about Brian's mom and Max, whose laughter intertwined in a distant harmony. They were probably in their own world, too, she thought.

Even through the layers of thick clothing, Jenny could feel Brian's warmth. She reached a tentative hand to smooth his damp, boister-ous curls, but Brian grasped her fingers and kissed them, one by one.

"Brian . . ." she whispered.

"Jenny." His eyes held her own. "I don't intend to be a secret to you any longer. Okay? From now on, I do all my admiring out front."

"What can I say?" Jenny couldn't stop smil-ing. Brian was everything she'd ever imag-ined him to be—and more.

12

Jenny was studying for an English test when the doorbell rang. She marked her place in her English text and went to answer it, thinking Evan would be there, ready to go running. She heard him playing the piano earlier, then stop, so she figured it wouldn't be long before he showed up.

"Brian." Jenny drew in her breath in surprise to see him.

"Are you going to invite me in, or leave me standing here on your doorstep?" he asked.

"C-come in," she stammered. "Obviously, I didn't expect you."

"Who were you expecting?" His eyes clouded momentarily.

"My friend Evan, my next-door neighbor, who is very anxious to meet you, by the way." Jenny showed Brian into the kitchen.

The whole family had gone to an air show in Watsonville, so the house was empty.

"Evan Cornell?"

"You know of him?" Jenny imagined how excited Evan would be that Brian knew his name.

"I've heard of him. He's on the track team."

"Yes. We run together, and that's why I'm expecting him." She made a quick survey of the refrigerator's contents. "Are you hungry?"

"No, thanks. But can I have a glass of milk?"

"Sure."

He was quiet for a moment, taking in his surroundings, focusing on Jenny's math paper, which was held on the refrigerator door by a magnet. "Your're a good student, I see."

"I try."

"Is Evan another one of your admirers?"

"No, Evan is a good friend of mine," Jenny explained, thinking how funny it was that Brian imagined she had lots of admirers. "You're the only one who's made a secret of himself."

"It's nice to stand out in a crowd."

She laughed. "Crowd? Oh, come on! If you only knew . . ." She shook her head in denial.

"I think I prefer ignorance, Jenny. Thank you very much." Brian leaned over and kissed her. He put down his milk glass and was about to put his arms around her when the doorbell rang.

"That must be your good friend," he said crossly.

Their eyes held for a moment before Jenny went to answer the door.

"Hi, Evan. I've got someone here I'd like you to meet." Jenny made sure she said it loud enough that Brian would be sure to hear.

"Yeah? Who?"

A perplexed Evan strode into the room. "Brian Halsey! Hey, I've been wanting to meet you for a long time."

"Same here." The two boys shook hands vigorously.

"Jenny's told me a lot about you." Evan winked at her. She couldn't help blushing.

"I guess I'm not such a secret after all?" Brian shot Jenny a teasing glance.

"Well . . ."

"You've had a pretty good track season this year, haven't you?" Brian went on talking to Evan, happy to converse about his favorite subject.

"Actually, since you've been out of the running, so to speak, we've been doing well against your alma mater." Evan laughed. "But the team knows it'll have to sharpen up before next season."

Brian laughed. "Seems to me I've seen you at a meet before."

"Yeah . . . you look familiar, too. Not surprising, huh?"

"I hear you and Jen are running today?" Brian asked.

"Why don't we show Brian our route, Evan?" Jenny suggested.

"Sure enough."

Evan led the way to the trail. Jenny and Brian followed more slowly.

"When I get past the hobbling stage, I'd like to join you guys. This is a great trail," Brian remarked enthusiastically as they made their way through the woods, still fresh from a recent rainfall. Leaves and branches were strung with jeweled raindrops that sparkled in the sunlight.

Jenny wandered ahead of the two boys. She could hear snatches of their conversation. It gave her a good feeling to hear them getting on so well. Brian stopped occasionally to rest, and Evan kept talking, telling Brian about his trip to Mexico City, Carlos's impending arrival and how he was looking into a summer job with the Flying Doctors, transporting medical supplies into small Mexican villages that never received medical assistance otherwise.

She thought back to the day she and Steve had walked down into the canyon behind her house, and how unhappy she'd felt while trying to convince him she still cared for him. That's not true anymore, she thought, smiling to herself, because everything's turning out okay. Maybe not quite okay—there were still remnants of her relationship with Steve to work out, but as Millie and Doris said, it was often difficult to keep a friendship after a romance. She hoped that wasn't always the

176

case. She hoped it would never be like that with Brian. Though she sensed that Brian was a lot different from Steve—easygoing, understanding, qualities she now realized were foreign to Steve, though he had others . . .

"What're you smiling about?" Brian was suddenly at her side, tugging playfully at the back of her hair.

"I'm smiling about how things are working out, and what a great day it is," she told him honestly.

"You're an optimist, is that right?" His blue eyes met hers.

"I think so."

"I think so, too." Brian slid an arm around her shoulders, one of his crutches dropping to the leafy forest floor as he did so. "Do you know how much you did for me while I was in the hospital?"

"Now, how would I know?" she demanded.

Brian threaded his fingers through her hair, drawing her close.

"Your face brightened my days, Jenny. Honest. I wished I could see it more often." He cleared his throat. "Maybe now I'll be able to."

"That shouldn't be too much of a problem," she said before her smiling lips met his.

Far off, they heard Evan's whistle—a birdcall that Jenny recognized. They used it in case they lost track of one another in the woods. "That's Evan," she whispered. "He probably thinks we're lost."

"Funny," Brian said. "I never noticed he was missing, did you?"

Jenny shook her head.

"Do you feel lost?" he asked.

"No. I know exactly where we are."

Brian kissed her nose, her eyelashes, her cheeks. "Whew. I had a feeling I was in good hands."

"I'm a candy striper, remember?" She giggled as she picked up his crutch and handed it to him.

"And maybe an ex-Girl Scout?"

"Uh-huh." She led him through the woods, calling for Evan through cupped hands.

Finally, Evan's freckled face appeared through dense foliage. "Oh, there you are. Thought I'd lost you," he grinned knowingly.

"We're not that easy to lose," Brian assured him. He and Jenny exchanged looks. Jenny felt overwhelmed; her heart so full, yet light with blossoming love for Brian.

"I'm going to jog ahead, if you don't mind," Evan said. "I'll see you up at the house?"

"We'll be there," Brian said, "though it may take us a while—" But Evan had already turned away and was soon lost to their sight.

Brian shifted his crutches and leaned toward Jenny. She could see the sunlight filtering through the leaves above his head and was conscious of his intent gaze before she closed her eyes to meet his kiss. "I'm glad you're not a secret anymore," she whispered as his lips grazed her cheek. "Very glad," she murmured, as his mouth found hers again.

"Jenny! It's me, Evan. You and Shelly must come over and meet Carlos, my friend from Mexico City."

"Oh, sure, Evan, we'd love to." She and Shelly were busy sticking stamps in their joint stamp collection when he called.

"Evan's Spanish accent has returned. Remember how he had it when he came back from Mexico City?"

"Yeah. I wonder if they want to help us with these stamps," Shelly said, sticking a bunch of them onto the end of her tongue. She then proceeded to do a dance around the room.

"I think you'd better not act like a weirdo in front of Carlos, Shelly. I mean, he's probably suffering from culture shock already. After meeting you, he might go home with some very strange stories."

"It will make his trip seem more interesting," she insisted.

Jenny picked up the sponge dish and the collection and put them on her desk. It was a project the two girls had started two years ago on a rainy day, when Jenny's father had received some car parts from Germany. Shelly had steamed the stamps off the packages, and later went home to find some Swedish ones she'd been saving. The next day they had bought a book.

"I wonder if Carlos runs," Jenny said as they walked over to Evan's.

"If he doesn't, he will by the end of his three-week stay," Shelly said.

Evan opened the door. Shelly stuck out her hand to Carlos, who stood behind his host. "Hi. Welcome to the United States," she said.

"Hi." Carlos seemed genuinely happy to meet the two girls. He listened carefully to Shelly's enthusiastic description of Jay and the baseball game they were going to later on.

"I would like to see beisbol," Carlos said in uneven English.

"Oh, great. Let's all go," Jenny said, anxious for an outing with Carlos. Once the weekend was over, and he was introduced to the entire student body, there wouldn't be much time to spend with the exchange student.

"Jay's the pitcher, which is a pretty important position," Shelly explained, pointing out her boyfriend, who waved at her. "Then there's the catcher . . ."

"I think Evan probably knows that already, Shelly," Evan said.

"Oh, Evan! He might not. And anyway, just in case he doesn't know, it's good to fill him in. I remember what it was like before I could understand football . . ."

Shelly described how she had cheered at all the wrong times during a football game. Jay had just about killed her because she cheered when the opposite team won, and she didn't live down her mistake for months. "It was even written up in the school newspaper," she told Carlos.

"Carlos, you're really lucky if you don't understand a word of that story," Jenny whispered to him.

"Why? Do you think it would be too much of a 'culture shock'?" he questioned, a teasing glint in his eyes.

"No question," Evan said. "You have to take Shelly by degrees. Don't let her overwhelm you the way she does me." He gave Shelly a friendly shove that nearly knocked her off the bleacher.

But Shelly was too absorbed to notice because just then Jay caught a fly ball, making the opposite team's first out. Shelly jumped up with excitement. "Yay, Jay!" she shouted.

Jay's team was now ahead. And by the end of the afternoon the Eagles had won the game.

Shelly was ecstatic. "I'm gong home with Jay, okay?" She hugged everyone, and waved goodbye. "Nice to meet you, Carlos. Maybe you can save us some stamps, huh?"

"Be happy to," he grinned at her as she bounced off down the bleachers to the playing field.

By the snack bar, Jenny saw Steve with a group of his friends. His eye caught hers in an instant and he turned away. How could he behave as though they had never been close?

She shivered. It was definitely time to set that relationship right. Everything else in her life was perfect: she had Brian's love, Brian was getting well, she and Shelly were pals again, but it was awkward because of Steve.

She watched him as he was swallowed up by the crowd. She thought of his interest in surf movies and all his good qualities about him that might be perfect for another girl, but were not right for her. She hoped that maybe someday she could tell him about them. She was unhappy about their misunderstanding and wanted to make it up to him somehow. Even though Evan had warned her that she and Steve would break up, she never anticipated it being this painful. How would she ever get through to Steve?

"Hey, Jenny! Jenny Carlson! Wait!"

At the sound of a familiar male voice, Jenny stopped in her tracks on her way out of the school's main building. Kids milled around, yelling and banging lockers—and the usual after-school pandemonium. She peered through toward the sea of heads at the boy advancing her through the mob.

"Hi, Steve. How are you?" she asked stiffly.

"I'm fine. Great, really. Do you have a second? I'd like to talk to you."

"Yeah, sure."

They walked outside. Thin sunlight had replaced a light, spattering rain. Even the quad, surrounded by bushes bearing those tiny red berries everyone threw at each other during lunch hour, sparkled as if it had been freshly scrubbed.

Steve stuck his hands in his parka pockets. His elbows waggled nervously. "I'm sorry for how I acted, Jenny, really I am. I like you a lot, and . . ."

His eyes told her how he felt—he kept glancing down at the cement, then back at her face.

"Hey, Steve, look. It's no big thing. I understand. Forget how you acted. I'm sorry for how I acted, too." She hoped he wouldn't sweat it. She'd certainly let herself worry about it for long enough.

"Yeah, well, I hate to have us part enemies, if you know what I mean. We were good together. We had a lot of fun, huh?"

"Yeah, we were, Steve. I had a lot of fun with you. You were my first boyfriend, you know." She smiled.

"I know. Well, look." He shoved a strand of bright hair from his eyes. "I just want to be friends. Do you think we can be?"

Jenny felt a wave of relief sweep over her at the sound of those words. She extended her hand to him and they shook on it. "We can be friends. I was hoping . . . that would be great, Steve."

"Gimme five," he said, laughing, and they slapped each other's palms, then said goodbye.

Watching him saunter across the quad, Jenny felt slightly sad. So it was really over—completely. Maybe there was no easy way to break up, ever. Maybe she'd always experience a tiny heartbreak when she saw him or heard his name.

"You'll get over it," Shelly had insisted, but

Jenny didn't know whether she could believe that or not. Shelly never seemed to fall very hard for any guy, even for Jay—and she was still bananas about him.

"You'll forget his name," she said, but Jenny had only laughed.

"Not if you're still my best friend, I won't." It would be impossible to forget Steve's name.

Then there was Brooke, who'd claimed she would never fall in love. How long ago was that? Two, three weeks ago? Time sure changes things. Little Brookie was all of a sudden crazy about a boy named Casey Maloney in her art class. She tied up the phone, engaged in long, intense conversations with him, and after talking to Casey, she'd call up one of her friends.

The blare of a horn interrupted her thoughts. Across the rain-jeweled lawn, Jenny spotted Brian waving from his bright yellow Lynx.

Holding her books close, she ran toward him, feeling like she could leap the distance in a single bound.

"Hi. How was school?" His smile warmed Jenny to the bottom of her toes.

"Oh, great. How was yours?"

"Fine. I didn't have to beat off the girls with my crutches today." Brian leaned over to kiss her, his cheek smelling faintly of aftershave. He brushed a strand of hair out of her eyelashes.

"Oh, too bad." She smiled.

"Hey, who was that guy you were talking to?" he asked, nudging her gently with his elbow.

Jenny smiled, threaded her arm through his and leaned close to his ear. "Oh, just an old friend of mine," she replied airily.

Four exciting First Love from Silhouette romances yours for 15 days—free!

If you enjoyed this First Love from Silhouette® you'll want to read more! These are true-to-life romances about the things that matter most to you now—your friendships, dating, getting along in school, and learning about yourself. The stories could really happen, and the characters are so real they'll seem like friends.

Now you can get 4 First Love from Silhouette romances to look over for 15 days—absolutely free! If you decide not to keep them, simply return them and pay nothing. But if you enjoy them as much as we believe you will, keep them and pay the invoice enclosed with your trial shipment. You'll then become a member of the First Love from Silhouette℠ Book Club and will receive 4 more new First Love from Silhouette romances every month. You'll always be among the first to get them, and you'll never miss a new title. There is no minimum number of books to buy and you can cancel at any time. To receive your 4 books, mail the coupon below today.

First Love from Silhouette® is a service mark and a registered trademark of Simon & Schuster.

First Love from Silhouette

THERE'S NOTHING QUITE AS SPECIAL AS A <u>FIRST LOVE.</u>

─── $1.75 each ───

- 2 ☐ GIRL IN THE ROUGH
  Wunsch
- 3 ☐ PLEASE LET ME IN
  Beckman
- 4 ☐ SERENADE
  Marceau
- 6 ☐ KATE HERSELF
  Erskine
- 7 ☐ SONGBIRD
  Enfield
- 14 ☐ PROMISED KISS
  Ladd

- 15 ☐ SUMMER ROMANCE
  Diamond
- 16 ☐ SOMEONE TO LOVE
  Bryan
- 17 ☐ GOLDEN GIRL
  Erskine
- 18 ☐ WE BELONG TOGETHER
  Harper
- 19 ☐ TOMORROW'S WISH
  Ryan
- 20 ☐ SAY PLEASE!
  Francis

─── $1.95 each ───

- 24 ☐ DREAM LOVER
  Treadwell
- 26 ☐ A TIME FOR US
  Ryan
- 27 ☐ A SECRET PLACE
  Francis
- 29 ☐ FOR THE LOVE OF LORI
  Ladd
- 30 ☐ A BOY TO DREAM ABOUT
  Quinn
- 31 ☐ THE FIRST ACT
  London
- 32 ☐ DARE TO LOVE
  Bush
- 33 ☐ YOU AND ME
  Johnson
- 34 ☐ THE PERFECT FIGURE
  March
- 35 ☐ PEOPLE LIKE US
  Haynes

- 36 ☐ ONE ON ONE
  Ketter
- 37 ☐ LOVE NOTE
  Howell
- 38 ☐ ALL-AMERICAN GIRL
  Payton
- 39 ☐ BE MY VALENTINE
  Harper
- 40 ☐ MY LUCKY STAR
  Cassiday
- 41 ☐ JUST FRIENDS
  Francis
- 42 ☐ PROMISES TO COME
  Dellin
- 43 ☐ A KNIGHT TO REMEMBER
  Martin
- 44 ☐ SOMEONE LIKE
  JEREMY VAUGHN
  Alexander

First Love from Silhouette

45 ☐ A TOUCH OF LOVE
Madison

46 ☐ SEALED WITH A KISS
Davis

47 ☐ THREE WEEKS OF LOVE
Aks

48 ☐ SUMMER ILLUSION
Manning

49 ☐ ONE OF A KIND
Brett

50 ☐ STAY, SWEET LOVE
Fisher

51 ☐ PRAIRIE GIRL
Coy

52 ☐ A SUMMER TO REMEMBER
Robertson

53 ☐ LIGHT OF MY LIFE
Harper

54 ☐ PICTURE PERFECT
Enfield

55 ☐ LOVE ON THE RUN
Graham

56 ☐ ROMANCE IN STORE
Arthur

57 ☐ SOME DAY MY PRINCE
Ladd

58 ☐ DOUBLE EXPOSURE
Hawkins

59 ☐ A RAINBOW FOR ALISON
Johnson

60 ☐ ALABAMA MOON
Cole

61 ☐ HERE COMES KARY!
Dunne

62 ☐ SECRET ADMIRER
Enfield

63 ☐ A NEW BEGINNING
Ryan

64 ☐ MIX AND MATCH
Madison

Lift Your Spirit This October With
THE MYSTERY KISS
by Elaine Harper

- -

FIRST LOVE, Department FL/4
1230 Avenue of the Americas
New York, NY 10020

Please send me the books I have checked above. I am enclosing $_____ (please add 50¢ to cover postage and handling. NYS and NYC residents please add appropriate sales tax). Send check or money order—no cash or C.O.D.'s please. Allow six weeks for delivery.

NAME _____

ADDRESS _____

CITY_____STATE/ZIP_____

First Love from Silhouette

Coming Next Month

The Mystery Kiss by Elaine Harper

Polly had been famous as a fortune teller ever since grade school. How come that the spirits wouldn't or couldn't tell her who had stolen that electrifying kiss from her on Halloween night?

Puppy Love by Janice Harrell

Brenda was determined to prove to Simon, her brother's best friend, that she was more than a pesky little sister or the neighborhood dog sitter. This turned out to be more of a challenge than either of them expected.

Up To Date by Beverly Sommers

No senior ever falls for a junior, all Wendy's friends informed her when she told them that she was sharing, of all things, a sewing machine with a cute guy in hom ec. Wendy didn't agree, and, fortunately, neither did Rick.

Change Partners by Sharon Wagner

When Kerri moved to a dude ranch in Montana she learned that there was more to it than helping to care for the guests and learning to ride. Two handsome guys were determined to rope her in. Which one should she choose?

Silhouette Romance

15-Day Free Trial Offer
6 Silhouette Romances

6 Silhouette Romances, free for 15 days! We'll send you 6 new Silhouette Romances to keep for 15 days, absolutely free! If you decide not to keep them, send them back to us. You pay nothing.

Free Home Delivery. But if you enjoy them as much as we think you will, keep them by paying the invoice enclosed with your free trial shipment. We'll pay all shipping and handling charges. You get the convenience of Home Delivery and we pay the postage and handling charge each month.

Don't miss a copy. The Silhouette Book Club is the way to make sure you'll be able to receive every new romance we publish before they're sold out. There is no minimum number of books to buy and you can cancel at any time.

READERS' COMMENTS ON FIRST LOVE BOOKS

"I am very pleased with the First Love Books by Silhouette. Thank you for making a book that I can enjoy."

—G.O.*, Indianapolis, IN

"I just want you to know that I love the Silhouette First Love Books. They put me in a happy mood. Please don't stop selling them!"

—M.H.*, Victorville, CA

"I loved the First Love book that I read. It was great! I loved every single page of it. I plan to read many more of them."

—R.B.*, Picayune, MS

*names available upon request